WORTH THE RISK

MIAMI SCORCHER SERIES

Savannah Stuart

Cover art: Jaycee of Sweet 'N Spicy Designs
Author website: www.savannahstuartauthor.com

Publisher's Note: This is a work of fiction. Names, characters, places, and incidents are either the products of the author's imagination or used fictitiously, and any resemblance to actual persons, living or dead, or business establishments, organizations or locales is completely coincidental.

Worth the Risk/KR Press, LLC -- 1st ed.

ISBN-10: 1942447221
ISBN-13: 9781942447221

eISBN-13: 9781942447214

This story is for Kari Walker. Thanks for being one of my biggest cheerleaders.

Praise for the books of Savannah Stuart

"Fans of sexy paranormal romance should definitely treat themselves to this sexy & fun story." —Nina's Literary Escape

"I enjoyed this installment so much I'll be picking up book one...worth the price for the punch of plot and heat."
—Jessie, HEA USA Today blog

"...a scorching hot read." —The Jeep Diva

"This story was a fantastic summer read!" —Book Lovin' Mamas

"If you're looking for a hot, sweet read, be sure not to miss Tempting Alibi. It's one I know I'll revisit again and again."
—Happily Ever After Reviews

"You will not regret reading the previous story or this one. I would recommend it to anyone who loves a great shifter story."
—The Long & Short of It

"...a fun and sexy shapeshifter book and definitely worth the read."
—The Book Binge

CHAPTER ONE

Stephan Lazos couldn't tear his gaze away from the exotic brunette moving across the dance floor below. From his position in the VIP room, he had a perfect view of almost the entire nightclub. The only thing he could focus on, however, was one woman. The wolf inside him wanted to throw her over his shoulder, take her out of the loudest club in Miami and back to his place for a marathon of fucking.

His skin tingled and burned as he watched her. The unwanted physical reaction was starting to piss him off. She was hot, sure, but she wasn't even his type. At six foot two, he liked his women tall and curvy. Once they got to the bedroom, he wanted a woman who had a lot of stamina and didn't mind the sex a little rougher. The woman on the dance floor looked as if she'd fall over if a strong wind came along.

Long, dark hair fell down her back in waves. It looked as if she wore three-inch heels, and she was *still* short compared to the blonde woman she was dancing with. Everything about her was petite and delicate. Each time her hips swayed in tune with the blaring music, her silky red dress shimmered around her tight body. And each time that happened, his cock jumped to attention. The primal beast inside him wanted to cover every inch of her exposed skin so no one else could look at her.

He liked sex as much as the next shifter, but this was *different* and he didn't understand his reaction. Since he was a pup, he'd never had to exert much mental control to keep his canines from extending. Now it was taking all his self-control not to *change.* And this couldn't have happened at a worse time either.

He was in the middle of an assignment. All his focus should be on convincing Antonio Perez that he was a new arms dealer in town looking to expand to medical supplies and *not* an undercover DEA agent.

"See something you like?" Antonio's voice caused him to step back from the balcony.

"I see a lot of 'somethings' I like," Stephan said as he took a sip of his scotch. The one thing he hated about this undercover role was his playboy image. The expensive suits and drinks were a nice change of pace from playing the role of junkie or hired thug, but the Miami party scene left a lot to be desired. One of his brothers owned a club downtown and Stephan had only been in it a handful of times.

"Anyone in particular?" the other man pressed.

Stephan couldn't afford to show any interest in one woman over another. There was no way in hell he could let Antonio think he had a weakness. "The group of women in the middle."

"I'll invite them up," Antonio said as he motioned to two of his bodyguards.

Stephan shrugged, as if it didn't matter one way or the other. However, his heartbeat quickened when the bodyguards ushered the group of barely dressed women up the stairs.

Her scent hit him with startling intensity. In this crowded, stifling atmosphere, his extrasensory abilities were working overtime. Alcohol, sex, the consistent thump of the bass from the speakers, it was overwhelming. Even so, he still knew the subtle jasmine scent that rolled over him was her.

Whoever *she* was.

As if she sensed him, she glanced around until their gazes locked. Her bright blue eyes widened when they made contact.

Mate.

The word echoed loudly inside his head. His heart skipped a beat at the thought. It was impossible that he would recognize her so soon. *Wasn't it?*

His brother Nick had told him what it was like when he'd met his mate, yet Nick hadn't realized Carly was his mate right away. He'd just been possessive and a little obsessed with her. Maybe in hindsight he should have realized. Of course Carly was human, not a shifter. But even his parents hadn't recognized one another right away. He'd always thought it would take time.

Mate. The word reverberated through him again. His wolf clawed at him, telling him to shut the fuck up; that was his mate. She was a wolf too, he could scent it. *All mine.*

Fuck, no. He refused to believe it.

He mentally shook himself, but his wolf just clawed harder.

Stephan had never imagined something being so physically overpowering that he couldn't think straight. And he definitely hadn't believed that he'd just *know* his mate on sight.

He set his drink on one of the high-top tables and started to make his way toward her. To his surprise, she flipped her dark hair over her shoulder in a haughty manner, turned her back on him and headed for the bar.

What the fuck?

He refrained from growling. Barely.

"Stephan, I have business to attend to." Antonio's voice pulled him out of his trance and back to the present.

The blaring music once again registered as he turned toward the drug-running asshole he needed to do business with. "So do I," Stephan murmured.

A lecherous grin spread across Antonio's face. "Good. Enjoy yourself. I must leave, but everything is still on for tomorrow?"

Stephan nodded. "I'll be there. I already have buyers lined up for most of your products. Your stuff better be as good as you promised."

He waved a hand in the air. "It's better. And I have a surprise for you. Not a product we discussed earlier."

"I don't like surprises."

"You'll like this one. Trust me. I will have women at the party, but feel free to bring some of your own."

Stephan waited until Antonio and his men descended the stairs before stalking toward the mystery woman. He'd been watching her out of the corner of his eye, and she hadn't moved from her seat at the bar. She was aware of him watching too, he was sure of it.

"Leave," he growled to the college-aged guy talking to her.

The blond kid started to say something then he must have recognized Stephan as one of Antonio's friends—or maybe he saw the rabid look in Stephan's eyes—because he mumbled something too low to hear and hurried away.

"That was rude." The blue-eyed beauty narrowed her gaze at him.

"What's your name?" he asked, ignoring her statement.

A small smile played at the corners of her very kissable lips. "Marisol."

Marisol. The name and her voice rolled over him. "I'm Stephan. Why are you out unchaperoned? What pack do you belong to?" Damn it, he hadn't meant to sound so harsh.

For a split second, her eyes flashed a darker shade of blue. She shrugged but he could smell her pain. She was decent at masking it, but it rolled off her in subtle waves. The very scent of it angered his wolf. Stephan had the most irrational urge to comfort her, even though he had no right to touch her. "I have no pack."

"Where are you from?"

She shrugged again. "None of your business."

He leaned in so that his mouth was inches from her ear. It took all his self-control not to nip or lick her soft skin. "It's most definitely my business."

She swallowed and he could sense her fear…and attraction.

Marisol Cabrera forced herself not to tuck tail and run. The wolf next to her was sexy as sin and he radiated dominance, but he was also a piece of shit arms dealer. In truth, she could let that go—and she wasn't sure what that said about her—but he worked with Antonio Perez.

That, she would never let go.

If she wanted to get out of this alive and to also complete what she'd come to Miami to do, she had to play this right. This male was very, very dangerous. Her inner wolf sensed it, even as she wanted to rub up against him. "And why is that?"

"You're my mate." His deep voice was like an unwanted aphrodisiac. Heat pooled in her belly.

Marisol wanted to deny it, but she'd sensed it on the stairs. She'd nearly tripped when she'd comprehended what was happening. She'd given up the hope or desire of finding her mate decades ago. Firsthand experience told her wolves could be just as treacherous as humans. She knew exactly who *Stephan Vasquez* was. She'd been watching Antonio Perez for months, waiting for the perfect time to get close to him before she ended his life.

And now she found out the man he'd been doing business with recently was not only a fucking wolf, he was her *mate*.

Unbelievable.

Fate was a cruel, cruel bitch and she'd certainly had a lot of fun torturing Marisol in the past year. Well, no more. Mate or not, she didn't care. It was only biology after all. Her body might want the man and the wolf, but she didn't love him, didn't even know him.

Considering what he did for a living, it was doubtful she ever would. She threw him a cool look. "So what if we're mates? I have a choice in the matter, you know."

He muttered something she couldn't understand. It sounded Greek, but she thought he was Cuban. Or at least that's what she'd learned through the grapevine. So many of the club-hopping South Beach girls wanted a piece of him. He was obviously rich and powerful, but he got that money through the pain of others. Marisol had only watched him from afar or else she would have known he was a shifter long ago.

She wasn't sure if that would have made a difference in her approach or not. Now she'd never know.

"Have dinner with me," he growled, taking her by surprise with his demand.

"Are you asking or ordering?"

He cleared his throat and she was under the impression that this was incredibly difficult for him. "Have dinner with me tomorrow night...please."

She set her drink down. "Maybe. Where are you going to take me?" She actually planned to say yes. Now that she realized how easy it would be to get to Perez through him, it was her only choice. Still, she wanted this sexy wolf to sweat it.

"I'll cook for you. My place."

She bit back a retort. Somehow she couldn't see this big man wearing an apron. He probably had a maid. But she needed him. "Are your sweaty looking thugs going to be there too?" She tilted her head in the direction of one of the men she'd seen hovering around him earlier.

His head swiveled around then he glanced back at her. It almost looked as if he'd forgotten they were there. "It'll just be you and me, *kardia mou*," he murmured.

She wasn't sure what the foreign words meant, but they sure as hell weren't Spanish. *Interesting.* "If you think you can handle me all by yourself, I guess the answer is yes." She uncrossed, then re-crossed her legs and took pleasure at the low growl she heard start to form in his throat. He had to smell her desire, no doubt about it. "You better watch yourself, *wolf*, or you'll change in the middle of this club."

She'd only been kidding, but his breathing became more labored and when she saw a flash of his canines, her heart rate increased about a hundred notches. Arms dealer or not, he was her mate and something primal inside her shifted at the thought of him in pain. She *had* to protect him. "Come on, let's get out of here." She slid off the stool and grabbed his hand, ready to bolt down the stairs she'd come up not long ago.

He had other plans. Stephan motioned to the men in suits to stay then practically dragged her toward one of the EXIT signs. Once they were in the private stairwell, he finally spoke, but his words were hoarse, animalistic. "I have a car waiting out back."

Something told her they weren't going to make it that far. So she did the only thing she could think of. Pressing her body against the full length of his, she wrapped her arms around his neck. If she could get him to stop from shifting she had to do it.

He didn't seem to need any more motivation than her body against his. His mouth slanted over hers with a rough, hungry intensity. As his tongue rasped over hers in erotic little strokes, she allowed her body to meld against his very hard one. She didn't want to want him, but her mind wasn't listening to reason right now as a rush of heat flooded between her legs.

She could feel the raw energy racing through him. All the hard lines and muscles of his body pulsed with excitement, mirroring her own reaction. The power of it rolled off him and coursed over her. Sometimes the urge to change could be overwhelming, but she hadn't had an issue controlling it since she was a pup. And something told her Stephan rarely had a problem with control either. At least she wasn't the only one so affected by this attraction.

She moaned when he nudged her legs open wider with his thigh. It had been so long since she'd let a man—or shifter—touch her, it was a wonder she didn't combust on the spot. Even though it was ridiculous, he felt somehow familiar, as if they fit perfectly. As their tongues and bodies intertwined, she inhaled his earthy scent.

When his cock pressed insistently against her lower abdomen, she moaned into his mouth. One of his big hands trailed down her back until it settled at the curve of her butt. He shoved the material of her dress out of the way so that he gripped bare skin. She shivered at the feel of his callused fingers.

"Fuck yeah, sweetheart." His voice was still a growl as he pulled back, feathering kisses along her jaw.

An inaudible sound tore from his throat as his fingers dug into her harder. Her inner walls clenched, desperate to be filled by this male, this stranger. She was ready to let him take her right up against the wall in this stairwell. Which was insane.

Before she got completely out of control she pulled her head back and pushed lightly at his chest. He was still breathing hard, but there were no signs of pointy canines and while his gaze was heated, his eyes didn't have that wild, uncontrollable look about them anymore.

"Are you okay now?" she asked. Hell, she wasn't sure if *she* was okay. She felt as if she could crawl right out of her skin and all they'd done was kiss.

"If I tell you no will you keep kissing me?" A trace of humor laced his deep voice, but his words were hoarse and forced.

Despite her desire to feel nothing for this man, Marisol could feel the corners of her lips pull into a smile. "You're not like what I expected," she murmured before she could bite the words back. She hadn't planned to let on that she knew what he did for a living, but now she couldn't take it back. He'd scent it if she tried to lie.

His gaze sharpened. "What do you mean?"

She shrugged out of his embrace and put some distance between them. "I *know* what you do for a living, Stephan Vasquez."

Something indefinable flashed in his eyes, but it was gone so quick she couldn't put her finger on it. Hell, she couldn't even smell the man's emotions. He was obviously very adept at hiding his true self.

"You don't know as much as you think you do, *kardia mou.*"

She rolled her eyes and forced her protective wall to slide back into place. This man was nothing to her. He was a means to an end. Once she completed what she'd come here to do, she didn't care if she lived or died. And she certainly couldn't allow some wolf to get in the way of her plans. "If you're fine, I'm leaving. This club is giving me a headache." Even though they were in the stairwell, the walls reverberated with the thumping music inside.

"I'll give you a ride." He took her by the arm in a possessive grip and started down the stairs.

She had no choice but to follow, but there was no way she was letting him give her a ride. "I'll take a taxi home, but thank you for the offer."

He grunted something under his breath as he held the door open for her. It emptied into an alley where a black SUV limousine with dark tinted windows waited. Before she could attempt to argue, he'd opened the back door and practically shoved her inside. "I told you—"

The door slammed behind him. "You're mine, and I take care of what's mine."

The slam lit the pilot light on her temper. *Arrogant bastard.* "We might be mates, but I haven't submitted to you," she snapped. And it was unlikely she ever would. The words remained unspoken but echoed through her mind. She was prepared to die to kill Perez, and she couldn't allow herself to be mated. Even if he was an arms dealer, to knowingly bond would be cruel to Stephan. Not all shifters mated for life, but werewolves did, and it was very rare to get a second chance if one mate died. If Perez figured out who she was, he would no doubt kill her and Stephan would likely never have the opportunity to mate again.

When she slid a few inches farther away from him, her dress shifted against the plush leather seat and revealed more skin. As if connected by a magnet, his eyes immediately strayed down, his look raw and sexual.

She'd worn the skimpy red dress to get attention. Of course, she hadn't wanted it from Stephan. She'd wanted it from Antonio Perez. The man was almost impossible to get to and she'd known she'd have to flash a lot of skin if she wanted to get invited to one of his parties. Now she had an even better way to get to Antonio and she wouldn't have to pretend to be interested in him. If she was Stephan's woman, he would have no reason to question her. "How long have you been doing business with Antonio Perez? I thought you dealt in weapons." And word on the street was that Perez dealt in drugs—legal and illegal. Guns and drugs were both bad businesses, but they weren't exactly the same beasts. For whatever reason, drugs brought more heat from the law in Miami.

A slight frown marred his handsome face. "How do you know about that?"

She shrugged. "Everyone in the South Beach circuit knows. You've been seen with him at all the clubs."

"Why haven't I seen you around before?"

Marisol inwardly cursed at how smoothly he changed the subject. "I'm not exactly a club girl. I was just out tonight with friends." It wasn't a complete lie. She'd been visiting clubs all over Miami for the past year trying to find a chink in Perez's security. The only time he ever let his guard down was around pretty women. So she'd befriended party girls. She didn't want the focus on her so she asked another question before Stephan could continue. "What pack are you part of? I haven't heard of any Vasquez's living around here."

"What *have* you heard?" He scooted an inch closer so their knees touched.

Her wolf sat up and took notice, wanting to feel more of the sexy male.

She started to answer when the window separating them from the driver rolled down. "Mr. Vasquez, where am I taking you?"

"My place in Key Biscayne," he ordered.

"No—" He pressed a finger over her mouth.

After the window rolled back up, she pushed at his shoulder. "You can't just take me prisoner. And you never answered my question. What pack do you belong to?"

"I'll answer your questions later."

"No. I want answers now. If you're not part of the Lazos pack, who the hell are you?" He was obviously an alpha, but something told her he wasn't an *Alpha*. He didn't run his own pack. No, he seemed like more of a loner. She'd heard that the Lazos pack made their home in Miami, but she'd never formally introduced herself to any of them or even sought them out. Miami was a big place and as a lone wolf, it had been easier than she imagined to blend in. Technically it was wrong, but at this point in her life, she didn't care about breaking some rules.

"You know about them?"

"I know that Miami is their home. I haven't met any of them. Are they okay with you being here?"

A small smile touched his lips. The action immediately softened the harsh planes of his face and she had the most irrational urge to reach out and cup his cheek. "I've spoken to their Alpha and he's allowed me to stay here as long as I respect his territory. Why haven't you introduced yourself?"

"I...truthfully, I hadn't planned to stay in Miami so long and I just never got around to it." Which was just a lame excuse.

"Don't you have any respect for our rules?"

He was one to talk. "Why are you taking me to your home?"

He sighed. "Are you always so difficult?"

"Only when I'm being kidnapped," she muttered.

He was silent so long she wasn't sure he'd respond. Finally he spoke. "Do you want to go home? I'll tell my driver to turn around right now."

She considered his offer for a moment. The truth was, she didn't mind going home with him. The closer she got to Stephan, the easier it would be to make her move against Perez. The nagging voice in her head shouted that betraying her mate was one of the lowest things she could possibly do, but she ignored it. Her family was dead because of Antonio Perez and if it was the last thing she did, she was going to put him in his grave.

Resolved, she hardened her heart and stared out the window. "I'll go with you."

CHAPTER TWO

Stephan shut the office door and fished his phone out of his pants pocket. His boss was going to be pissed when he realized he'd ditched his team, but he didn't want anyone knowing about Marisol. That included *everyone* he worked with. Luckily he'd convinced his boss to hire a private limo company as part of their cover. And that company just happened to be owned by his Uncle Cosmo.

He was taking a big risk bringing her to one of his family's beach houses instead of the place the DEA was using for this operation, but he needed absolute privacy. His cover house was bugged in every room and he'd made sure Antonio Perez knew about its location. Letting the other man think he knew of his whereabouts had gone a long way in establishing trust between them.

Sighing, he dialed the number.

Reuben Woods, Director of the DEA's Miami division, picked up on the second ring. "Where the fuck are you?"

"I can't talk."

"Coleman said you left with a woman. Who is she?"

"I can't say."

"What the fuck does that mean, you can't say?"

"You're just gonna have to trust me. Saturday is still a go, so make sure a team is ready."

"We are. Are you under duress?"

"*No.* Trust me."

There was a long pause. "All right. Check in with me tomorrow morning."

Stephan disconnected then took the battery out of his phone. His phone was already encrypted but he wasn't taking any chances Woods would try to track him. Woods was a good guy, but Stephan had only worked with him a couple times and at this point, Stephan didn't trust anybody. Not with his mate. Most of his assignments had been out of state and that was the way Stephan liked it. Working jobs too close to home made him feel uneasy. His family could take care of themselves, but it lowered his stress level just the same. He'd made an exception for this case.

He knew his boss would be pissed the next time they talked, but hell, Woods was lucky they were even in communication right now. While they'd played this case close to the chest and only a handful of people knew about it, normally Stephan went in undercover with one contact and one contact *only.* It helped eliminate leaks that way.

When he heard a soft knock at the door, he slipped the phone and battery into the top drawer of the desk.

All the muscles in his body tightened when he opened the door to find Marisol standing there. The animal in him wanted to strip her naked and fuck for hours. And her outfit wasn't helping matters. The shirt stretched across her small breasts, perfectly accentuating her soft curves and hard nipples. It was too short though, and it exposed the lower half of her flat stomach.

"This sort of fits." She tugged on the hem of the black t-shirt he'd given her.

"It covers more than that dress you were wearing." Stephan heard the possessive note in his voice but couldn't stop himself. Didn't care at this point. All his wolf knew was that she was his mate.

"Whose clothes are these anyway?" She narrowed her bright blue eyes at him, a sudden pop of annoyance rolling off her.

"I've never slept with the woman they belong to if that's what you're asking." The skintight t-shirt and yoga pants he'd given her belonged to his cousin Alex. He knew because he could still smell traces of her in the house. His answer was evasive but it wasn't an outright lie. More than anything he wanted to tell Marisol who he really was, but he couldn't yet. Mate or not, he didn't know anything about her and he sensed she was holding something back from him. The fact that she didn't have a pack—or rather claimed not to have one—set off alarm bells.

The house they were in was one of his parents' extra beach houses they reserved for visiting wolves or friends of the human variety. It was rarely used so he'd known it would be unoccupied and better, it wouldn't have any family photos lying around. His pack was very particular about not keeping personal photos around their own homes, much less a guesthouse.

She placed her hands on her hips and the haughty expression on her face got him hotter than he could have imagined. "So what do you plan to do to me now that you've got me here?"

"Talk." He wanted to do a hell of a lot more than talk, but he needed to know who this sexy she-wolf was and why she hadn't introduced herself to his Alpha sometime over the past year.

"Talk?" Her voice was disbelieving. The sweet jasmine scent he'd noted at the club was more potent and enticing here at the house.

"Do you want a glass of wine?" He needed to keep his hands busy with something other than her. If he didn't, he was likely to take her right on the floor. With the way she'd been grinding up against him in that stairwell, he was pretty sure she'd let him.

Without answering, she turned on her heel and headed for his kitchen. Watching the subtle sway of her hips had his cock on full alert and his brain barely functioning.

He easily caught up to her as they entered the kitchen. Everything in the house was state of the art, but it was also very sterile. It felt like a hotel and probably fit in with his profile as an arms dealer. He hated that she thought he sold weapons for a living.

"Shouldn't you have more security or something?" Marisol asked.

"No one knows about this place. Besides, do you really think I'm worried about getting killed?" Unless someone shot or poisoned him with silver, he was pretty much indestructible.

A soft smile tugged at the corner of her very kissable mouth. "Good point." She slid onto one of the high-top bar stools at the center island while he pulled a bottle from the wine rack along the wall. When she moistened her lips with that perfect pink tongue, he had a sudden vision of her running that tongue over his cock and he nearly dropped the bottle.

"Is red okay?" When she nodded, he poured them both a glass and sat next to her. With his loud family, he normally liked silence, but the quiet room left him nervous.

Nervous.

The word was laughable. He'd never felt insecure around a female—wolf or human—in his entire life. Most of the time he could smell their desire, fear, whatever. People were easy to read.

Not Marisol.

He couldn't tell if she was purposefully hiding her feelings or if she was just private. The only thing coming off her was jasmine and need. Even if she wanted to, she couldn't hide her desire for him. On his most primal level, that pleased him.

The silent tension in the room swelled until the air was thick with his desire mixed with hers. He knew it was biological and he also knew it was what happened when one met their mate, but he didn't like feeling such little control over his body.

After taking a few sips of her wine, she set it down on the marble countertop. Her intelligent eyes studied him carefully. "What are you thinking?"

"You probably don't want to know," he muttered, even as he wondered exactly the same thing. He wanted to know what was going on in her head.

In a surprising move, she slid off the chair and positioned herself between his legs. His cock jutted forward when she lightly pressed her fingertips against his chest. The challenging look in her eyes was unexpected.

Instead of kissing her, he threaded his fingers through the curtain of her dark hair and grasped the back of her head in a tight grip. The strands were silky and cool against his palm. "What are you playing at?" A growl rumbled at the back of his throat.

"You don't want me?" she practically purred. Her hands settled on his thighs and she raked her fingernails teasingly along his legs.

Against his will, his leg muscles clenched under her light touch. God help him, he wanted her. More than he cared to admit. It had been a while since he'd been with a woman. Ever since his younger brother had found his mate, sadness and a touch of jealousy had settled deep inside Stephan. He wanted what Nick had so he'd basically turned down any woman he met. "Don't play games with me."

"I won't let you bond with me, but I want you." The truth was in her words and in her scent. Her desire grew stronger with each second that passed.

He'd been ready to bond since practically the second he'd seen her, but it was the female's right to choose when and where they would bond. He wanted to take Marisol right on the kitchen floor so badly his cock ached, but his human side won out. Unable to voice his intentions, he hooked his hands under her ass and picked her up. Immediately she wrapped her slim legs around his waist. Her erotic scent enveloped him in a thick cloud. Wordlessly, he strode for the master bedroom. They might not be about to bond, but they were certainly going to fuck.

CHAPTER THREE

Marisol knew she was playing with fire, but Lord, she wanted this sexy shifter. If she was going to die, she was going to enjoy life before she did. Fate might have been cruel enough to lead her to her mate now, but that didn't mean she couldn't take some pleasure.

She felt as if she were in heat, she was so hot. She needed relief and she needed it *now.* Rubbing her breasts over his chest, she grinded against his body as he carried her from the kitchen. She sensed he was worried about her sudden change of heart. It wasn't as if she'd planned to sleep with him tonight, but she wasn't going to deny herself what she wanted. Especially when she knew he'd get just as much pleasure. It was a win-win for both of them.

Her surroundings vaguely registered when they entered a large room. Strange, the bedroom didn't smell like Stephan. It didn't smell like anyone. It simply smelled like fresh, clean cotton. She was glad that it didn't smell of another female.

Marisol was more than comfortable with her body, but she was thankful when he didn't turn the lights on.

It had been a while since she'd had sex and the last man she'd contemplated letting into her bed had tried to kill her.

The floor-length curtains were drawn back on the wide window, allowing the moon to give them just enough light to see each other. While shifters didn't need a full moon to shift forms, the sight of it always pleased her inner wolf, soothed her.

When her feet touched the floor, she tried to step back but hit the edge of the bed. The heat of Stephan's body wrapped around her was sensual and enticing. Instinctively, she curled her toes into the plush throw rug in anticipation of what was to come. The dark look in his eyes told her she wouldn't be disappointed. He murmured something low and unintelligible as he grasped the bottom hem of her shirt. Her stomach fluttered in response.

Her vision was bathed in darkness for a moment as he lifted the shirt over her head. Cool air rushed over her skin, causing her already hard nipples to pebble even more.

She reached out to touch his muscular chest, but before she realized it, she was flat on her back and he'd pulled her stretchy yoga pants completely off. She'd ditched her thong earlier and by the heated, primal look on his face, he was pleased. He'd be able to scent her desire as well, no doubt.

A strange shyness threatened to overwhelm her, and that wasn't like her. But she was naked and completely at his mercy. The thought was startling.

While she was a lot stronger than she looked, she was no match for this man. In wolf or human form, this man—her mate, could hurt her if he wanted. He wouldn't though. She could feel it straight to her bones. He might make a living peddling weapons, but he didn't hurt women. Somehow, she just *knew* it.

"I don't have condoms," he rasped out, breaking the silence of the room.

She understood what he was asking without him actually having to voice it. Shifters didn't need protection because their DNA was different than that of humans. They couldn't get STDs, which meant they couldn't give them. And female shifters could only get pregnant twice a year. Thankfully, she was three months away from her cycle. "Don't worry, it's not my time—"

Her words were lost as he crushed his mouth over hers. In erotic little flicks, his tongue danced against hers. She briefly wondered what it would feel like to have him kiss her pussy like that. The erotic image that conjured brought a rush of heat to her belly.

As if he read her mind, he tore his mouth away from hers and carved a heated path of kisses along her jaw and neck. Continuing, he moved down her chest and stomach until he hovered at her mound. Oh yeah, he didn't waste any time getting to exactly where she wanted.

Grinning wickedly, he buried his head between her legs. On instinct, she lifted her hips to meet his mouth, wanting everything this male had to offer right now. He dipped his tongue between her folds and licked her slit from the bottom, up to her clit. When he traced his tongue around the sensitive nub, her hips rolled against him.

"Stephan." His name fell from her lips as a ragged moan.

She wasn't exactly sure what she'd been expecting from him in the bedroom, but it hadn't been *this*. Everything about Stephan was big and demanding. The man exuded absolute power. She'd thought he'd take her from behind, needing to dominate her. She'd been so sure that he'd fuck her long and hard in that typical shifter way.

This, however, she could handle. *This*, she wanted more of. With a tenderness she hadn't expected, his tongue stroked between her pussy lips before focusing on her most sensitive bundle of nerves. He gently teased her with his teeth and tongue, the alternating pressure driving her crazy.

She slid her fingers through his hair, digging into his head, and grinding against his face. She felt absolutely possessed. "Oh yeah, just like that."

He growled against her and she could scent his pleasure to her reaction. With each flick against her clit, her hips jerked wildly. He chuckled against her most sensitive flesh. The reverberations skittered over her skin, sending spiraling tingles straight to her aching nipples.

Her legs automatically tried to clench around his head, but he pressed calming hands to her inner thighs. The feel of his touch immediately relaxed her in a way she hadn't expected.

Unexpected tears sprang to her eyes at the gentle way he handled her. It had been so long since she'd let her guard down with anyone and the tenderness from this man was almost overwhelming. The energy coming off him was raw and primal, but he was restraining himself. For her.

She didn't know him, but he was her mate and that obviously meant something to him. It meant a lot to her too. A year ago, she'd have opened her arms to him and bonded with him before falling in love. A year ago she'd been so secure in who she was and her place in the world, that she'd have known that the love would eventually come with the mating—that nature would work itself out. A year ago, she'd been stupid and naïve.

Stephan ran his hands along Marisol's inner thighs and savored the feel of her soft, smooth skin. When he'd first seen her at the club he'd assumed she was delicate.

She might be soft and petite, but he could sense the unleashed power humming through her. She was strong. Stronger than maybe *she* even realized, and it made him want her even more. He couldn't believe that yesterday he hadn't known this woman existed and now here she was about to come apart against his mouth. And he'd make damn sure she came, over and over. The need to make sure she was sated consumed his wolf, demanding he take care of his mate.

Dipping his tongue into her pussy once again, he groaned as he tasted her sweet essence. Each time he traced his tongue along her slick folds, her hips jerked. She was so sensitive. Like dynamite.

Mine. The word was loud in his head. Like he needed the reminder from his wolf.

More than anything his cock wanted inside her, but he was going to play this right. Something told him she expected him just to fuck her like an animal, and he wanted to give her enough foreplay so she never wanted to leave his bed. The more he touched and kissed her, the more the desire to bond took over. The need ran deep inside him, coursing through his veins with a rampant, wild intensity. He needed her to submit and accept his dominance.

Something was holding her back though. The fact that they were mates wasn't enough for her. He could sense it.

So he'd bind her with sex until her human side came around if that was what it took. Not that having endless hours of sex with this little vixen would be a chore. Just the thought of that and his hips jolted forward once.

He focused on her pulsing clit. Circling it with the tip of his tongue, he traced it over and over again until her entire body was trembling. He knew she enjoyed it so when she removed her hands from his head, he risked a quick glance up to find her fisting the sheets underneath her. Her head was thrown back, her eyes were closed and her body was stretched out like an offering. And for the moment, she was all his. A low groan rumbled in his chest.

He was thankful he was still dressed or he'd have just pounded into her, claimed her. *Focus.* He looked back at her swollen lips, mesmerized by the erotic sight before him. Her clit peeked out, just begging to be kissed some more. Sucking the glistening pearl into his mouth, he took pleasure when she moaned and arched her back against his kisses.

She was so close to finding release. He could feel it in every tight line of her body. Removing one of his hands from her inner thigh, he teased her entrance with his finger. As he rubbed her, she scooted closer, as if trying to force his finger inside her.

No way, sweetheart. I say when. He withdrew his hand and fisted her hips before tugging her ass closer to the edge of the bed.

Her head immediately snapped up. "Are you stopping?" she gasped. Her blue eyes shone bright in the light from the moon.

His throat clenched as he tried to find the words. *Any* words. "Not on your life," he managed to rasp out. He couldn't have stopped, even if he'd wanted to. She was his mate and his body wouldn't let him forget that.

She looked so beautiful stretched out on the bed. Never before had he felt so possessive, so greedy about a woman. He was possessive by nature, but he'd rarely felt jealous with the women he'd been with. As he stared down at Marisol, he couldn't imagine letting her go. For two werewolves to mate, there was supposed to be a choice. It was against their laws and against nature, but a male could technically impose his wants and take the choice away from the female. Any man who did that was a piece of shit. That was something he could never do to Marisol. She was his mate and even though the wolf inside him wanted to claim her, mark her for his own so the entire world would know she belonged to him, he couldn't take away her choice. He might be part wolf, but his human side ruled him.

He inserted one finger then two inside her wet sheath and shuddered when she clenched around him.

She was so tight. It had obviously been a long time for her. His wolf and human side practically growled with satisfaction.

As he slowly dragged his fingers in and out of her, he reveled in the tiny moaning sounds she made. Each time he pressed against her inner wall, she tried to squeeze her thighs around him.

Her legs were bent and her feet were positioned at the edge of the bed, completely spreading her sweet folds open for him—silently begging for more. She painted such an erotic picture it was hard to concentrate on what he was doing.

"Touch yourself," he ordered hoarsely.

Without pause, her hands strayed to her breasts. His balls pulled up painfully as he watched her movements. She cupped both breasts then started strumming her nipples lightly with her thumbs.

Keeping his fingers between her legs, he continued sliding in and out of her then sucked her clit into his mouth.

The sharp, almost abrupt action had the intended effect. Her hips pitched forward so he increased the movements of his fingers. Her inner walls clamped wildly around him.

"Stephan," she moaned.

Just hearing his name on her lips was a turn-on. As he licked and circled her hardened bud, she pushed over the edge.

With a cry, she threaded her fingers through his hair as her body was overtaken with racks of pleasure. He could actually feel her orgasm roll over him. He wasn't sure if it was a mate thing or if they were just physically in tune. Whatever it was, it was hot as hell.

When her climax hit, she came long and hard and clenched even tighter around him, drenching his fingers with her slickness. As she came down from her high, she pushed up on her elbows and met his gaze, her breasts rising and falling with her panting breaths.

Pure satisfaction flowed through him at the blissful expression on her face.

"That was... I don't know...that was..."

"I hope the end of that thought is good," he murmured.

She laughed so lightly it was almost a giggle. Even though she was delicate and feminine and he barely knew her, the sound seemed foreign coming from her. Something told him she rarely laughed.

"Yes. Good. Very good." She got up onto her knees so that he got a full view of her naked body. He wasn't sure what she planned, but when she grasped at his belt and started unhooking it, he tugged his shirt over his head and tossed it across the room.

CHAPTER FOUR

Marisol's breath caught. She'd known he would look amazing, but his broad chest, ripped abdominal muscles and lean waist made her mouth water. She frowned when her gaze rested on a scar across his chest. It took a lot for werewolves to scar. The jagged wound was old but it looked as if it had been painful at one time. She placed a gentle hand over the faded white marking. "How old are you?" she whispered, not wanting to break the quiet of the room.

"One-hundred-sixty-eight." His voice was equally low.

Almost seventy years older than her. "When did you get this?"

He cleared his throat. It was obviously a painful subject for him, but he answered. "Vietnam."

"This must have hurt," she murmured.

He nodded and muttered something under his breath. She wasn't sure what to make of his admission. The man ran guns, but he'd cared enough to fight for his country at one time in his life. Interesting. And confusing.

"Stop thinking." His deep voice brought her back to the present.

She smiled and actually obeyed. He was right, thinking was overrated. She just wanted to feel tonight. Leaning forward, she pressed her mouth to his chest.

His muscles bunched under her touch. Knowing she had the ability to make this huge man shudder was an incredible turn-on.

After tracing her tongue around his small brown nipple, she took it between her teeth and tugged lightly. He actually jumped at the action. Lifting her head, she met his gaze. "You like that?"

"Yes." The word tore from his throat. She bent to kiss him again, but he grabbed the back of her head in a dominating grip and crushed his mouth over hers. He definitely liked to be in control, something she could get used to.

As his tongue danced with hers, her hands wound their way around his neck and she was flat on her back once again. This time, her sexy wolf was on top of her.

She rubbed her breasts against his bare chest. The soft thatch of his dark hair stimulated her already sensitized nipples. The orgasm he'd just given her had been good, but she wanted more. She wanted him inside her and more than anything, she wanted that elusive emotional connection she'd lost during the past year. It had been impossible to let anyone get close to her while on her mission, but being with him now, she realized how lonely she'd been. He'd been so giving and she wanted to make sure he found as much pleasure as he'd already given her.

He pushed up and immediately she mourned the loss of his mouth. He was in tune with what she wanted though because he finished what she'd started earlier and shucked his pants.

His cock sprang free and she involuntarily gasped. It had been longer than she cared to admit since she'd let a man in her bed, and he was long and thick. So very thick.

Before she had too much time to dwell on his size, he covered her body once more as he sought out her mouth. She knew it was crazy, but kissing him somehow felt familiar. Right even. She really *really* didn't want to care or think about the future, but allowing a man like Stephan into her bed was something she could get used to.

Pulling back from her just a fraction, he smoothed a hand over her hair. "Where'd you go just now?" he murmured against her mouth.

"What?" she whispered back. His tenderness tangled her up inside.

"You're thinking of something else." His breath tickled her skin.

She wanted to deny it, but the words stuck in her throat. Luckily, he didn't expect a response. He feathered light kisses along her jaw and earlobe until he centered on her neck.

She shuddered when he raked his teeth over her skin. Her neck tingled and burned with a desire to be claimed. Her entire body was screaming that this was her mate, but she simply couldn't submit to him. If she allowed him to pierce her skin, marking her as his own, they would be bonded for life and—no! She couldn't allow her thoughts to drift in that direction. It was pointless and it wouldn't be fair to him anyway.

When his head dipped to her breast, all those thoughts fled like dry leaves in the wind. He traced his tongue around her nipple in the same erotic motion he'd teased her clit. She was helpless to stop the way her entire body quivered. Instinctively she wrapped her legs around his waist and arched her back, lifting into him.

For a moment, he raised his head. "Are you ready?"

She nodded because she didn't trust her voice.

"Say it," he persisted, his gaze locked on hers. Oh yes, he was very demanding.

"Yes."

He briefly tested her pussy with a finger then pushed his cock into her with one hard thrust. Her inner walls expanded and tightened around him as she adjusted to his size. Instead of pounding into her, as she'd expected, he stayed immobile and bent his head back to her breast.

Why did he have to be so damn nice? So tender and gentle? He was making it much harder to think of him as an arms dealer who just happened to be her mate. Her heart squeezed.

She tensed as thoughts of a future with him entered her mind. They could have a family. She wouldn't be alone anymore. She could love someone and they'd love her back. Her life could be different. A burst of hope surged through her, but it was quickly doused with reality. She wasn't going to get a chance to have a family or a future. She didn't deserve it.

He must have sensed her distress because he lifted his head again. "Am I hurting you?"

"No, not even close."

In response, he began moving inside her. He kept his movements fluid and controlled. His neck muscles corded tightly and the raw energy rolling off him was unmistakable.

The man was definitely controlling himself and she found that it pleased her immensely. She locked her ankles behind his back and met him stroke for stroke.

His cock hit her deep inside and each time it dragged against her G-spot, she thought she'd explode. She was so close to climaxing again, she couldn't believe it. She just needed a little more stimulation.

Propping up on one elbow, he hovered over her and flicked and teased one of her nipples with his thumb. When he took her other hardened bud between his teeth and tugged, she lost it.

Her entire body felt overly sensitized. On one level she understood that they were mates but she couldn't understand how this virtual stranger had learned what her body needed so quickly.

The sweetest sensation surged through her. She ran her hands down his smooth back and clutched his backside in a tight grip as a forceful climax built and peaked. When she dug her fingers into his taut skin, it was as if she set him free.

Clutching the sheet next to her head, he shuddered as he emptied himself inside her. Over and over, he thrust until he finally spent himself. With a loud shout, he collapsed on her, melding his body to hers.

She threaded her fingers through his hair with one hand and gently stroked along his back with her other. His muscles clenched under her soft touch and she could feel his erratic heartbeat against her chest.

After a long moment, he groaned and rolled off her. Before she could protest, he disappeared into the bathroom.

Sighing, she lay against the pillow and stared at the ceiling. Getting tangled up with this wolf was probably the dumbest thing she could have done, but it was so hard to care when her body was completely satisfied.

She glanced up when he returned. Frowning, she nodded at the cloth in his hand. "What's that?"

"I told you I take care of what's mine." He sat on the edge of the bed and before she could guess what he meant to do, he reached between the juncture of her thighs and cleaned her. The soft stroking was soothing and as pleasurable as it was unexpected. Her whole body sighed at the consideration he showed her.

No! She refused to fall under his spell or to even dream about a future.

When he was finished he tossed the cloth onto the floor and slid into the bed next to her. Without a word he pulled her so that her back was against his chest. The curve of his body was so warm and strong. His breathing was slightly labored and she could feel his cock lengthening against her back.

Thanks to biology, shifters were able to have sex for hours on end. He was obviously ready to go again, but she wasn't, and it surprised her that he wasn't pressing her for more. It made her throat tighten.

If someone had asked her a day ago what she thought about Stephan Vasquez, she would have had a sure answer. Now she realized she didn't know anything at all and that terrified her.

CHAPTER FIVE

Marisol's eyes flew open with a start. She glanced around the foreign bedroom and frowned when she realized she was alone. The espresso colored silk sheets were rumpled next to her, but the bed was otherwise empty. And Stephan wasn't in the connected bathroom either. She knew because she couldn't smell his scent. Last night had been amazing and it surprised her that she wanted to see him again so soon. She'd been waking up alone for the past year with no one to care if she lived or died.

She slipped out of the huge bed and walked to the window. Her eyes widened as she took in the landscape. The night before she'd been too wrapped up in Stephan for her surroundings to even register. In addition to a private dock, a boat—scratch that, *a yacht*—a perfectly manicured lawn and an Olympic sized pool, Stephan had a completely unobstructed view of the ocean. Calm, glistening and expansive—the teal-blue water seemed to stretch out forever.

It was a little chilly out, but she'd love to try his pool. Then her stomach rumbled, and she realized how hungry she actually was. Casting a backward glance at the pool, she tugged on the clothes he'd given her the night before and went in search of Stephan. She still couldn't believe she'd found her mate in a Miami nightclub of all places. Even though she wanted to call what they'd shared the night before simply sex, she couldn't.

He'd taken such gentle care with her, it was frightening. She didn't want to care for this man. Didn't want to feel anything. Somehow he'd gotten under her skin without even trying.

Her feet were quiet along the hallway runner, the stairs and the wood floor that led to the kitchen. The aroma of rich hazelnut coffee and something—*someone*—tickled her nose. Whoever she scented was female.

Her canines tingled in annoyance. Marisol frowned as she stepped into the kitchen. "Hello?" She nearly jumped back when a tall—very pretty—redhead popped up from behind the large island in the middle of the room.

The redhead's blue eyes widened. "Hi…who are you?"

Marisol didn't sense any danger from the woman, but she was surprised at the jolt of jealousy that shot through her. Why the hell was another woman in Stephan's house? Before that thought had fully formed another scent hit her with startling intensity. This woman was marked by someone and it most definitely wasn't Stephan. Marisol's jealousy instantly dissipated.

"You're human," she blurted out before she could censor herself. She hadn't even realized humans and werewolves could mate.

A curious smile played across the woman's face. "A few months ago, I might have thought you were crazy if you'd said that to me… I'm Carly by the way. Are you friends with Nick's parents or something? Alisha said I could stop by, but she didn't mention anything about anyone being here."

"Uh, who are Nick and Alisha?"

The redhead's mouth pulled into a thin line and a wave of blatant distrust rolled off her. "Who are *you*?"

Marisol opened her mouth, though to say what, she had no idea. The sound of a door handle jiggling stopped her. She turned to find a completely naked Stephan walking in from the backyard.

"Oh my Lord! I don't want to see that!" Faster than Marisol would have thought possible, Carly threw a dishtowel at Stephan and covered her eyes. "For the love of God, cover yourself!"

To Marisol's surprise, his neck and face turned four shades of red. "What the hell are you doing here?" he muttered.

"Your mom sent me over to grab candlesticks for Nick's birthday thing. Which by the way, you still haven't responded to… Are you covered yet?"

He shot Marisol a guilty look and cleared his throat. "Yeah."

Carly dropped her hand and glanced back and forth between Stephan and Marisol with narrowed eyes. "Why are you staying at the guesthouse? I thought you were out of town or something."

"Guesthouse? You don't live here?" Marisol asked.

"Not exactly," he muttered.

"Are you related to him?" Marisol directed her question to Carly because she had a sneaking suspicion that Stephan had been holding back a lot from her.

Carly nodded. "He's my brother-in-law—"

"Damn it, will you just stop?" Stephan thundered.

Both women turned to stare at him.

"I'm sorry, I didn't mean to yell. I just...ah, damn it." He raked a hand through his dark hair and cursed under his breath.

This woman was mated to a werewolf and as far as Marisol knew, only *one* pack lived in Miami. If Stephan had lied about where he lived... "What's your last name?" she asked Carly.

The pretty woman bit her bottom lip and cast a nervous glance at Stephan, but she answered. "Lazos."

Marisol swiveled to Stephan who held his hands up in defense. When he did, he dropped his towel.

The redhead averted her eyes again. "Oh for the love of… I'm leaving…it was nice to meet you, uh, what was your name?" she asked Marisol.

Despite the barely leashed anger humming through her, she gave the other woman a tight smile. "I'm Marisol."

"It was so nice meeting you. Sorry about barging in. I didn't mean to interrupt anything…okay, then, I'll…" Oversized candlesticks in hand, she brushed past her and hurried from the room. Her heels clacked against the tile of the kitchen and echoed as she moved throughout the rest of the house.

When Marisol heard the front door slam, she blindly reached for one of the coffee mugs on the counter and hurled it at Stephan. She'd had enough wolves lie to her to last a lifetime. "You lying son of a bitch! Is this some kind of game?"

"I can explain!" He ducked out of the way and the mug smashed against the wall.

Before the broken shards had even hit the floor, she picked up another mug. As she hauled back to throw it, he grabbed her and held her arms by her side. Using the extra body weight he had on her, he shifted positions and pinned her against the island counter.

Despite his strength, she struggled against him. "Let me go, you bastard!" she shrieked. Against her will, a sob tore from her throat and tears started to fall. Everyone was a liar! *Even her mate.*

"Don't cry! Shit, *kardia mou,* don't cry." He started to loosen his hold but when he did she got an arm free and punched at his chest.

There was no give to the broad expanse of his muscles, but it made her feel better. Since he wasn't holding her legs, she lashed out and kicked him in the shin. He winced but she doubted it even fazed him. "You lying piece of shit! I'm leaving." She tried to kick him again, but he hooked his much larger leg around the back of her knees, immobilizing her. She wiggled again. In that instant, she hated how short she was. If she could just get a leg free...

"I'm an undercover agent for the DEA!" he shouted in her ear.

She stopped fighting and her head snapped up at the admission. "What?"

"Fuck. Fuck, fuck, fuck!" He released his grip and pushed away from her.

Stephan turned his back to Marisol. He was in such deep shit he couldn't even wrap his mind around it. This woman might be his intended mate, but that didn't matter. He didn't know anything about her. It was doubtful, but for all he knew, she was a mole for Perez.

When she'd said she was leaving, something inside him had snapped. He couldn't lose her. Not when he'd just found her.

He swiveled back to face her. She still stood next to the island. Her hands were clasped so tightly in front of her, her knuckles had turned white. They faced off, neither saying anything. Hell, he didn't know where to start.

Finally she broke the silence. "So, you're not an arms dealer, huh?" Her quiet voice seemed overly loud in the even quieter room.

"Nope."

"How do I know you're telling the truth?"

"Why would I bring you to my family's home? When I realized who you were, I wanted to keep you safe. Stephan *Vasquez* doesn't care about women, but Stephanos *Lazos* cares about his mate. I couldn't let Perez know you meant anything to me so I brought you here. I sure as hell didn't plan for you to meet my sister-in-law."

She stared hard at him for a moment then nervously rubbed her hands over the front of her pants. Even though she held his gaze, a light blush of pink stained her cheeks. "Sorry about your coffee mug."

"That's the least of my worries," he muttered. He might have just screwed up one of the biggest takedowns he'd ever been involved with. It had taken decades to find a job he enjoyed. Hiding the fact that he was a werewolf was hard enough. He wasn't even sure how he was going to tell his boss that his cover was blown.

"I'm not going to tell anyone." Her voice was barely a whisper.

"What?"

"I won't... I'm not going to tell anyone who you are if that's what you're worried about. There's no one I could tell even if I wanted to."

Her last statement caught his attention. "What pack are you from? No lies."

"Tell me about yours first...please." The pleading note in her voice tore at his gut. Standing in front of him, she suddenly looked lost and impossibly young. By shifter standards he guessed she was close to a hundred, but she looked to be about twenty-two. Without the makeup she'd had on last night, she *barely* looked that.

"My real name is Stephanos Lazos. I hail from Leontio, Greece, though I haven't lived there for over a century. My father, *my Alpha,* is Lucas Lazos, my mother is Alisha, and my two brothers are Thomas and Nicolas—Nick for short. You just met his new wife, Carly. She's one of the few humans who know about us. For now we call Miami home but we'll probably move in a decade. I have a lot of cousins, but there are too many to name. Your turn."

She bit her bottom lip as she assessed him. He felt as if he were under a microscope, but if it got her to talk, he didn't care about the scrutiny. "My last name is Cabrera and my entire pack is dead. I'm originally from Asuncion, Mexico, but my Alpha moved us to northern California when I was a pup. We moved around but I had never left the state...until a year ago when I came to Florida. I literally have no one in my life so you have nothing to worry about from me."

"You have me." The words slipped out.

Disbelief flitted across her face, but it happened so fast and then her protective mask was back in place. Her pain and loneliness tore at his insides. He couldn't keep his distance any longer. Closing the gap between them, he wrapped his arms around her and pulled her into a comforting embrace.

At first she tried to pull away, but finally she wrapped her arms around his waist and laid her head against him. She was quiet, but he could feel the wetness of her tears on his skin. His chest tightened as the thick shroud of her emotions surrounded him.

A dozen questions raced through his mind—like why the hell was she in Florida and why had her entire pack *died*? Even though he needed to ask them, he knew *she* needed to be held. Whether she admitted it or not. His protective instinct kicked into overdrive as she pressed her lean body against his.

He searched for a way to distract. "You want to go for a run?" he murmured into her hair.

"Is it safe?"

"My pack owns a private stretch of beach here. That's where I just came from."

She pulled her head back to meet his gaze. Her eyes glittered with unshed tears but there was a hopeful spark in her eyes. "I'd love to."

She stepped away from him and stared at him expectantly. His older brother, Nick, had connected telepathically with his mate after the first time they'd had sex, but Stephan couldn't link with Marisol. Or maybe she was intentionally blocking him out. Either way, he wished he knew what was going on in her head at that moment.

"Uh, it's this way." He motioned toward the back door.

Tentatively she followed him. When they were outside on the stone patio and she didn't make a move to shift, he realized she might be shy about undergoing the change in front of a stranger.

He didn't have a lot—or any—modesty, but she was in a new area with someone she barely knew. Hell, she'd lost her entire pack. That was something he couldn't even fathom. Without his family, he'd go crazy. It was a wonder she hadn't.

Wordlessly he turned and changed forms, hoping to give her some privacy and to let her see him at his weakest moment. As his bones shifted and broke, then realigned, the pain hit with the intensity of a tsunami. While the pain was inevitable, it was always fleeting. It quickly faded until he felt nothing more than pleasurable tingles along his spine.

In wolf form, his auditory senses were amplified a hundred fold. Behind him, he could hear her clothes hit the ground then he heard her sharp intake of breath before she made the change herself.

Before he could turn, he felt a cold nose against his fur. When he turned to look at her, he growled protectively. It shouldn't surprise him, but she was a small wolf. Maybe seventy-five pounds and her shifted form was that of a brown and white Alaskan malamute. She was...cute. It was the only word to describe her.

She nudged him again and yipped playfully. In response, he trotted across the patio toward the open stretch of sand. Instead of following, she ran a few feet ahead then turned to face him. With her paw, she kicked up the grains in his direction and yipped again.

Follow me, he projected with his mind, but she didn't seem to understand. His pack could communicate telepathically in wolf form and while it was just a pack thing, he'd thought it might be possible with Marisol since they were mates. Hopefully after they bonded they'd be able to communicate that way.

She crouched down on all fours as if ready to attack but her tail wagged playfully. When he bounded toward her, she leapt away from him and ran toward the ocean. Keeping his pace slower so he wouldn't scare her, he followed suit and let her lead the way. He liked this side of her. She was definitely easier going in wolf form.

As they ran along the beach, he let go of his earlier worries. He'd have to face them eventually, but for now he let the salty essence of the ocean envelop his senses while he enjoyed this time with his mate.

CHAPTER SIX

Marisol forced herself to relax as the shower jets pummeled her shoulders. She guessed the bathroom had been custom designed because everything in it was higher and wider than normal and very expensive looking. The marble shower—which was big enough for four people—and matching oversized tub had the splendor of the old-world. Combined with the dark cabinets and warm fall colors of the room, it was actually very inviting. Traditional in style.

The run with Stephan earlier had been exhilarating, but now she had a bigger dilemma. Stephan wasn't the asshole she thought he was.

He was a freaking DEA agent. He was one of the good guys.

Which meant he wanted to arrest Perez. She didn't want the man behind bars though, she wanted him six feet under. He was an absolute monster. Now she wasn't sure what to do. One part of her wanted to tell Stephan what Perez was capable of, but she worried he'd try to keep her away from him. What was she thinking, of course he would. He was a male shifter and her mate. Males were always so damn protective.

She couldn't afford that. Not when she'd come so far. Not when she was so close.

Stephan's earthy scent tickled her senses. He must be close by. As soon as they'd returned from their run she'd changed back to her human form then darted off to take a shower. She knew he had questions but she wasn't prepared to answer them so she'd run away like a coward. She should have known he'd follow.

Her eyes were closed as the water rushed over her body, but she knew he was in the bathroom now. He wasn't making a sound, but she could practically feel him in the room with her. Maybe it was the mate connection because she swore she felt him caressing her skin. "Why don't you just get in here?" she asked.

"I am." She opened her eyes at his deep voice. He was right in front of her and she hadn't even heard him approach.

"You're very quiet," she murmured.

"That's because I'm the big bad wolf," he growled playfully.

She liked this side of him, even though part of her wished she could still view him as an arms dealer. Still holding the sudsy loofah in her hand, she shifted out of the way so he could join her under the water.

As he stepped under the steady stream, he reached for her hips, but she swatted his hands away and swept the loofah over his chest and stomach.

A soapy river trailed down his chest and her gaze couldn't help but follow it. His cock twitched as she drank in the sight of him.

"Are you just going to stare, or are you going to touch?" His deep voice brought her gaze back up with a start.

Stephan's dark eyes glittered with barely contained lust. Without responding, she set the loofah on the built-in bench and knelt in front of him. She was most definitely going to touch all she wanted. He was like a tasty piece of candy and she was going to savor the time she had with him.

Grasping his cock at the base, she ran her clasped fist up the length of him, then back down again.

"Marisol." Her name tore from his throat on a groan as he pulsed in her tight grip.

She risked a quick glance upward. His eyes were closed and his chest rose and fell rapidly. She loved being able to make him pant. Grinning in satisfaction, she leaned forward and licked the underside of his thick shaft. She kissed and nibbled along his length. Each time her lips or tongue touched his cock, she could feel almost imperceptible tremors racing through his body.

All the muscles pulled tight in her body as she licked him. Knowing she could bring him pleasure made her ache with an undeniable need. He'd taken so much care the night before making sure she found release, she wanted to do the same for him.

Keeping her hand tightly around the bottom of his cock, she wrapped her lips around his crown and sucked lightly. Thick and long, the man was a freaking fantasy.

"Oh yeah," he murmured, sinking his fingers into her hair and tightening on the strands with a gentle pull.

Those two words were all the incentive she needed. She traced her tongue around the crown before taking him fully in her mouth and sucking hard. With her free hand she played with his balls, lightly tugging on them while she continued working his cock with her mouth. When his hips started gently thrusting, and he moaned out her name over and over in a sort of prayer, her nipples hardened in response.

Water rushed down her back and over her chest but she could barely feel it. All she cared about was getting him off. Bringing him pleasure was suddenly the most important thing. It was totally primal, but this was her mate and she wanted to hear him crying out her name. She didn't have to wait long.

His cock jerked in her mouth and she realized he was close to coming. When his grip tightened on her hair, she increased her movements.

Her fist squeezed and pumped faster as she sucked him harder. And that was all it took.

"Gonna come." His voice was hoarse. "Marisol, shit..." Another groan wrenched from him.

She rarely swallowed, but she wanted—no, needed—to taste him. It wasn't lost on her that he gave her the opportunity to pull back either. But moving away was the last thing she wanted. She placed a hand on his thigh for support as he exploded in her mouth.

His come hit the back of her throat in long, hard jets. Keeping her lips firmly around his cock, she continued sucking and kissing him until he sagged against the wall.

She lifted her head and couldn't stop the smile spreading across her face. He looked so satisfied, it was hard not to feel pleased with herself. His dark gaze sought hers out and before she realized what he planned, he hooked his hands under her arms and lifted her up.

As his mouth crushed over hers in a demanding, erotic dance, he fisted her hips and pulled her roughly against him.

She clutched his shoulders for support and when he tugged her bottom lip between his teeth, she arched her back. Tingles shot down her spine and the ache between her legs grew with each second that passed.

It had been so long since she'd been with a man and she'd thought last night would quench her thirst. Instead she was primed and ready to go for hours and hours. Even her breasts were heavy with need, every single part of her body over sensitized.

His hands began a slow trail up her waist until they settled right under her breasts. He cupped them and in unison, rubbed his thumbs over her nipples.

Desire coiled in her belly. She desperately needed to find release; her wolf was clawing at her in demand. When she groaned into his mouth, he pulled his head back a fraction.

"What do you want, *kardia mou?*" His breath was a whisper over her swollen lips.

"I want you inside me." She spoke softly, not wanting to break the intimacy of the moment.

His eyes flared with white-hot lust at her declaration. Immediately, his hands strayed from her breasts and around her back. He grasped her ass and squeezed lightly. When he did, her inner walls tightened. She savored the feel of his fingers caressing her wet skin, even as she wanted more.

"Hands on the wall," he murmured, sending more shivers skittering across her skin, straight to her toes.

"What?"

"Now." The word was a subtle order.

She instinctively clenched her legs at the command that resonated through his voice. Slowly, she turned around and placed her hands on the cool tile.

"Now spread your legs." He hadn't shaved that morning so his stubble tickled her neck when he spoke close to her ear.

His cock pressed against her back and when she did as he ordered, a cool draft rolled over her slick folds. They were already swollen with need and he hadn't even touched her.

When she felt his mouth on her shoulder, she tensed for a split second as she wondered what he would do. But he didn't attempt to mark her. He simply feathered kisses along her back.

The trail led straight to her ass. He pulled away so that neither his mouth nor hands were touching her. She couldn't see him, but she knew he had to be kneeling behind her. He was able to see every little imperfection about her. She was spread open for him and she was suddenly very aware how much at his mercy she was. If he wanted to claim her, bond with her, he could. Her instinct told her he wouldn't without her permission, but a sudden dose of fear poisoned her thoughts and her muscles tightened.

She started to close her legs when he dipped a finger inside her. At the same time, he raked his teeth over her behind and her body pushed her insecure thoughts away. So far Stephan had been nothing but giving and kind. She was so wet it was almost embarrassing. Her slickness flowed freely over his hand and down the inside of her thighs.

His finger felt good, but she wanted a lot more. She needed his cock to fill her, stretch her, take her. "I want *you* inside me."

"Soon." He continued teasing her sheath for a moment before trailing his finger back to her tight rosette. She clenched as he pressed his finger against it. The thought of letting him touch her there was surprisingly erotic. Especially since they barely knew each other.

"Relax." Again, his voice was commanding.

Braced against the wall, she trembled. He wouldn't hurt her. She was sure of it. If she told him to stop, he would. Forcing her body to listen, she imagined what it would feel like when he once again filled her. When she exhaled a long breath, he slipped his finger into her hole. Her head fell back on a soundless cry at the foreign, yet erotic sensation.

In her hundred years she'd never let a man touch her back there. She'd never had the desire to. Now she wondered why she'd waited so long. The slight stretching filled her with indescribable pleasure.

He continued pushing into her with slow measured movements. Her body clenched around his finger and her inner walls spasmed out of control, wanting to be filled. This male knew exactly how to make her crazy.

"You're so tight." His deep voice sounded strained.

Her breath caught as he penetrated deeper. The building ache threatened to make her lose her mind.

Desperate for relief, she reached between her legs and touched herself. Gently rubbing between her swollen folds and over her pulsing clit eased the ache some, but she still needed more. She needed Stephan.

Without warning, he withdrew his finger and seized her hips. Before she had a chance to prepare herself, his cock plunged inside her. Her inner walls stretched and expanded, but in this position it was easier than the night before to take his size.

He reached between them and ran his callused palm over her ass, tracing a finger down her cleft. This time she wasn't nervous when he slid a thick finger inside her tight rosette. A soft moan escaped her lips. "Stephan…"

With wild and almost uncontrolled thrusts, he rocked into her. The rougher movements were different from their first time yet her body felt on fire. It was almost as if her skin burned for his touch everywhere. Her ass clenched around his finger as her pussy clamped around his cock.

It was too much to take. Bending forward a few more inches, she moved her hips back against his, meeting his insistent strokes. Every time his shaft slid into her, she pushed closer to finding her release. Combined with the steady probing of his finger, she finally pushed over the edge in a soundless wave of ecstasy.

Her mouth opened, but no sound came out as a violent jolt of pleasure rippled through her core. It started between her legs and pushed outward, moving across her belly and breasts. The climax built and built until it felt as if she could actually explode from the pleasure. She reached out to hold onto something but the tile was too slick and her knees felt like rubber.

Stephan could feel Marisol's body contracting around his finger and cock simultaneously. It took all the willpower he had not to come again. She might not realize it, but he wasn't done with her yet. Not by a long shot.

He needed to bind her to him and he planned to do that in the most primal way possible.

As she rode through the last part of her orgasm, her legs gave way. Hooking his free hand around her waist, he pulled her up so that her back pressed against his chest.

Slight tremors raced through her body. Strange that he could feel the tremors almost as if they were coursing through him. He bit back a groan as he slowly withdrew from her. His own body screamed for release, but this was about her. She turned around on unsteady legs so he kept his arm hooked around her waist.

"Are you okay?"

"More than okay." She laughed lightly. "That was...amazing."

Pure satisfaction filled him. He didn't know how he knew, but she'd never allowed a man to touch her the way he had. Later, when they knew each other better and she completely trusted him, he wanted to use more than his finger. "I'm not through with you yet."

"You're out of your mind." She pressed a weak hand to his chest, but he turned off the shower and grabbed a towel.

She was silent as he rung the dampness out of her hair. When he finished drying her, he picked her up and carried her to the bedroom.

Before her back had hit the sheets, he claimed her mouth in a possessive, demanding kiss. He loved taking her from behind, but he loved kissing her even more. She had a distinct, sweet taste that was something purely hers.

Even though he'd just been inside her, he wanted more. As he stretched out on top of her, he covered her mound with his hand and played with her clit. She'd just come, but he simply wanted to touch her, bring her as much pleasure as she could handle.

She arched her back against him so he bent toward her chest. When he drew her ripe nipple between his teeth and pressed down, the doorbell rang.

Marisol tensed underneath him. "Are you expecting someone?"

Sighing, he stopped sucking her breast and laid his head on her chest. "No."

He wasn't expecting anyone, but that didn't mean his family wouldn't stop by unannounced. Now that they knew he was here and that he'd brought a woman to one of the family homes, they'd be stopping by to check her out. His pack was just nosy like that. If he had to guess, he'd say one of his brothers was at the door.

Or his Alpha.

CHAPTER SEVEN

Antonio Perez pressed his hand to the biometric scanner and waited for the solid steel door to open. Seconds later, it drew back with a whoosh.

Dr. Reed looked up as Perez entered the sterile room. "You're just in time. This latest strain is showing more promise than the others."

Antonio looked through the glass at the two subjects chained down. "How are the subjects fairing?"

"These two are stronger than the other werewolves. The small one is doing the best. She's...different. Her blood is different from the other one. It's working better with the mutation."

Antonio narrowed his gaze at the petite Spanish woman chained down. *Woman.* That word was laughable. The werewolf before him had so much unleashed power and he planned to share that power with governments willing to pay enough. If it wasn't for the sedatives pumping through her system, he had no doubt she'd be able to break through her restraints.

With the right formula, he was going to create super soldiers. But first, the drugs needed to be perfected. "How did the human test subjects fair with this strain?"

"It's only been a week but one male subject is adapting perfectly. His DNA is bonding with the formula and his strength has tripled. No side effects either. He's the exception though. The others...weren't so lucky. However, it's my opinion that the current group of humans is too weak. If we're going to truly examine the possibilities, I need men who are physically above average. Their bodies will go through an extreme transformation and they need to be able to handle it."

"You'll have your men. Vasquez is coming tonight. Will everything be ready?"

The doctor shifted from one foot to another. "Possibly."

"What the hell am I paying you for? You've had years to perfect this! We've finally found the perfect werewolves. Vasquez has the contacts I need. If I renege on this, he'll kill all of us! Maybe I should find someone more willing—"

"No, no, everything will be ready." He shuffled away, mumbling to himself as he peered into one of his microscopes.

"It better be." Perez dealt in heavy quantities of drugs but as a very lucrative arms-dealer, Vasquez had the contacts he needed and Perez couldn't afford to make him wait. It wasn't as if he could call up third-world dictators or other heads of state and schedule a meeting. No, something like this would require a go-between.

Someone respected and feared would need to introduce him and Stephan Vasquez was just the man.

Antonio had no clue how the doctor's mind worked and he really didn't care, so long as he gave him what he wanted. Before leaving the lab he strolled to the thick two-way window and raked his gaze over the two naked subjects. They were different in physical appearance but both equally stunning. One was a petite brunette with perfect round tits any man would enjoy. The other was tall, blonde with a body made for modeling. That was what she'd done at one time. Now she was just another missing person.

The two before him were his favorites so he was thankful they hadn't died during the experiments. Kidnapping them had been time consuming and expensive, but after he'd killed the males of their packs and poisoned the females with smaller doses of silver, it had been easy enough. Even though they couldn't internally ingest it without getting sick, for some reason, silver bonds had a calming effect on the werewolves. In addition to the drugs he was giving them, they were helpless.

As if she knew she was being watched, the petite brunette with the midnight black eyes turned to stare at him. It was impossible that she could see through the mirrored window, but she glared directly at him nonetheless. He walked a few feet to the left and her eyes followed his movements.

His skin crawled under her scrutiny and he could actually feel himself getting weaker. It made no sense, but he had the strangest desire to open the door to her cell. An intoxicating sluggishness flowed through his arms and legs, as if he were stoned. Antonio walked toward the door, but the doctor's nasally voice dragged him back to reality.

"Yes, yes. We are almost ready," he muttered.

He looked back at Doctor Reed who was mumbling to himself as he jotted down notes.

"I'll be back this afternoon. Make sure the drug and the video is ready." Without waiting for a response, he hurried from the room. Anger hummed through him as he strode through his house. He wasn't sure what the hell had just happened in there, but he knew one thing. Once they'd gotten what they needed from the pretty werewolves, he was going to fuck that dark-haired one long and hard before he killed her. He might even keep her around as his slave for a while. He'd give the blonde to his men. So many of them had already shown interest, it would be a shame to let that body go to waste.

* * *

Stephan didn't bother looking through the peephole. He knew who was on the other side before opening the door. He pulled the heavy oak door open to find Thomas waiting.

"Hey, little Brother. I hear you've got company." A tired smile lit up Thomas' normally unreadable expression.

Stephan stepped back to let his brother inside. "I guess the whole family knows I've got a she-wolf here?"

"Nope. Just me." Thomas' shoes were silent as he stepped onto the tiled foyer.

"Carly didn't tell everyone?"

"Nah. She told Nick, who called me."

Relief rolled over him immediately. "I thought for sure she'd have called mom by now."

"I think she wanted to, but Nick stopped her."

Stephan bit back a smile. He couldn't be certain, but he was fairly sure Carly was still pissed at him for keeping her mate away from her all those months ago. It had been necessary at the time—and only a couple days—but she hadn't seen it that way.

Thomas continued. "So who is she?"

He glanced back at the stairwell. It was empty. "Her name is Marisol Cabrera... She's my mate."

Thomas' dark eyebrows shot up. "You're sure?"

"Yes."

His brother's lips pulled into a thin line. "Cabrera, why does that sound familiar?"

"I still don't know much about her, but she's without a pack. She said her pack died."

"How?"

"She didn't say."

"And you didn't ask?" Thomas' gravelly voice was incredulous.

"It's complicated."

"*I'll bet.* You stink of sex. Is the reason you haven't asked because you haven't come up for air?"

Stephan growled at his oldest brother who only laughed.

Just as suddenly, Thomas' face sobered. "Cabrera... Dad said their Alpha wasn't at the last Council meeting and no one has been able to contact any of their pack since."

Stephan frowned. The last Council meeting had been almost six months ago. Packs from around the world met twice every year to get updates on one another, to hold trials for rogue werewolves and to handle any general business. It wasn't unusual for some Alphas to occasionally miss a meeting, but they always sent someone in their stead. "I'll speak to her about it today."

"See that you do. Dad will want to meet with her soon."

Stephan bit back a sharp retort. The protectiveness humming through him was expected, but if what his brother said was true, Marisol would have to come up with an explanation for why her pack had suddenly died and she was still alive. He'd just been avoiding the fact. "I know."

"Why not bring her to Nick's birthday party on Wednesday? It'll give her a chance to meet everyone. She can talk to dad before the party starts."

It was Saturday. Four days should be enough time to convince his intended mate to tell him the truth about what had happened to her pack. It wasn't that she'd outright refused, but it had been obvious she hadn't wanted to tell him. While he didn't want to push, he had no choice. "We'll be there…if you could keep it under wraps that I'm staying here—"

"I won't let mom find out."

"Thank you." With the exception of his cousin Phillip who'd driven him the night before, no one knew he was staying at the guesthouse. Well, now Carly and his brothers knew too, but that didn't bother him. The one person he really didn't want finding out was his mother. She'd been hounding Carly to have children for months and if she discovered he'd found his mate, there would be no end to her interference. It wouldn't matter that it was loving and with good intentions, it would still drive him insane.

After his brother left, he started up the stairs only to find Marisol descending them. "I was just coming to find you. That was my brother."

"Oh." Her cheeks tinged a dark crimson and from her guilty scent, he guessed she'd been eavesdropping. "I need something to wear other than this." She motioned to the t-shirt and yoga pants.

Even though all he wanted to do was strip her naked and *keep* her naked, he knew she was right. She needed clothes and he needed to call his boss. "Grab your dress and shoes. I'll call my driver and we'll head to your place in a few minutes."

Wordlessly she nodded and hurried back up the stairs. Once she was out of sight, he headed to the office and called Reuben.

He answered on the second ring. "Hey." He definitely didn't sound as angry as he'd been last night. That had to be a good sign.

Stephan just hoped his boss was feeling generous this morning. "Listen, I know I acted unprofessionally last night but I ran into a family friend at the club. She was about to blow my cover so I had to leave with her."

"Shit," Reuben muttered.

"I've explained things to her and she'll be staying with my family the next couple days so there's no chance of her relaying the information to anyone—not that I believe she would anyway. Still, it's a risk so if you want to call off the operation, I understand." He couldn't tell his boss the entire truth, but it pacified his conscience somewhat to tell him they'd been compromised.

"No, we've worked too hard to bring Perez down. You sure she'll keep her mouth shut?"

"Positive—and she won't make any unsupervised phone calls anyway. She's tight with my family, it won't be an issue." He cringed at the lie, but there was no other way.

"Do you think we should put her under protective custody?"

"No. That'll just scare her. Besides, the meet is tonight—and it's my ass on the line. I trust her." The fact that his boss had even asked as opposed to telling him, meant he didn't want to go through the hassle of putting someone under protective custody. If they did, more people would be privy to their operation and that meant a greater chance of a leak.

"All right. As soon as you hear from Perez, contact me and you better get back to your cover house. He's got men watching the place and it'll look odd if you don't show up."

"I've got a few things to take care of but I'll be there this afternoon." He needed to explain to Marisol why he needed her to stay at his family's beach house tonight as opposed to her own place. They had a good security system and more importantly, he was going to have one of his brothers stay with her to keep an eye on her. It wasn't as if he could bring her to Perez's home.

"See that you are."

As soon as they disconnected, he scrubbed a hand over his face and sighed. He'd finally met his mate and it couldn't have come at a more complicated time in his life.

CHAPTER EIGHT

Marisol glanced over her shoulder, worried that Stephan would check on her. After tossing half her closet into her suitcase, she grabbed her pistol, extra ammunition and the printed layout of Perez's home she'd acquired. She quickly tucked the weapon into the bottom of her bag.

She'd tried telling Stephan she'd be fine staying at her apartment, but he'd been absolutely unwilling to listen. Not that she was actually complaining about that part. The sex with Stephan was like nothing she'd ever imagined.

She rolled her luggage into the living room to find him sitting on her couch. The tufted loveseat hadn't been made for comfort and with his big size, he looked incredibly uncomfortable.

"I've got all my stuff." For some reason, having him scrutinize her place made her nervous. When she'd moved to Miami, she hadn't planned to stay as long as she had and decorating hadn't been high on her list of things to do.

He stood and immediately reached for her suitcase. Instinctively, her grip on it tightened, but she forced herself to let go. She reminded herself that he wasn't planning to dig through her things, he was just being a gentleman. He was acting like a mate.

As he started to roll it toward the door, she cleared her throat. Even though she desperately wanted to get him out of her place, she still had unanswered questions. "Why can't I stay here tonight?"

"I'll tell you once we're out of here."

"No. I want to know *now*." She sat on the edge of the couch and crossed her legs. The temperature had dropped considerably since yesterday so she'd put on a tight turtleneck sweater dress with knee-high boots with four-inch heels. She didn't miss the way his gaze lingered on her legs and she also couldn't help the way her panties dampened at the evident lust in his dark eyes. This mating pull was insane. She'd never really believed the attraction could be as intense as this. Whatever she'd thought in the past, she hadn't even come close to the reality.

"I can throw you over my shoulder, Marisol." His voice was wry.

"You could, but I won't make it easy for you. Do you really want people paying attention to you? Remembering you were here?" She couldn't bite back a grin at his annoyed expression. He might be an alpha wolf but so was she. She didn't take well to orders, even if they were from her mate.

He swore softly under his breath and released her luggage. "I'm meeting with Perez tonight and in case things go wrong, I don't want you here alone. It's doubtful he even knows we left the club together, but I won't take the chance."

"You're meeting with him? What does that mean?" Her heart quickened.

"I… I can't tell you."

"Why can't I go with you?" she persisted. If he was meeting Perez, this was the perfect opportunity for her to get to him.

"You just can't."

"So you're going to go party with him and a bunch of his whores and you want me to stay home? If that's how you treat your mate—"

"Damn it, Marisol! You know that's not what I meant. This is my job."

Wordlessly she stood and strode past him. Something told her that no matter how much she gave him the silent treatment, it wouldn't matter. She needed to devise a plan to make him listen to her. It sounded as if tonight's meeting was important and it might be the only chance she ever got to kill Perez. If only she could convince Stephan to let her go with him. No, that would never work. He was in protective mate mode. She'd just find another way to get to Perez.

She was silent as they made their way to the elevator and once they were cruising down the road in his dark SUV, she finally broke the silence when it was obvious he wasn't planning to. Apparently this male was stubborn. "Is tonight's meeting important?"

"Very." A simple, one-word answer.

She tapped her finger against the center console and gritted her teeth. If he didn't want to talk, that was fine with her. She'd been living by herself for the past year with no real friends. It was a little depressing, but she'd gotten used to silence.

Palm trees and cars whizzed by as he headed toward Key Biscayne. She hadn't realized how close downtown Miami was to the barrier island. Before she realized it, they were pulling down the long private driveway of his beach house. He hadn't said it outright, but his pack had to have a lot of money to own a private stretch of beach in south Florida. *A lot.*

Hers had done well enough for themselves and she'd managed to leave California with a large chunk of funds but nothing compared to what the Lazos pack must have. She couldn't help but wonder what Stephan's real place looked like and what he must have thought of hers. All the furniture she'd gotten at second-hand stores and she didn't live in the best part of town—

"Stop, you're killing me," Stephan muttered.

"What?" She shot him a quick glance.

"Whatever you're feeling insecure about, just stop…please. It hurts."

"You can read my mind?" She'd heard of mates being linked telepathically, but they hadn't bonded so she'd assumed it wouldn't happen.

"No. I can feel your insecurities." He reached out and squeezed her hand.

Of all the things he could have done or said, that surprised her the most. She froze for a moment but didn't pull away. Touch was something she'd desperately craved over the past year. Her pack had been big and loud and often obnoxious, but she'd loved them. She missed her oldest sister's laugh more than anything. Marisol had been the youngest of three girls and her sisters had always looked out for her. She hated that she hadn't been there for them. Hadn't been able to stop what that monster had done to her whole family. She didn't know where that bastard wolf who'd betrayed them to Perez was, but she knew where *Perez* was and that was good enough for her.

"Fuck," Stephan growled as he threw the SUV into park.

"What?" she gasped as his hold on her hand tightened.

Stephan unstrapped his seat belt before releasing Marisol's restraint. Whatever was going on in her pretty head was nearly killing him. His chest tightened in absolute agony. She was such a mystery but now he knew without a doubt that she kept a lot of pain and misery locked inside. He didn't know much about comforting the opposite sex. Sure, his younger cousins sometimes came to him for advice, but this was different. He wanted to take all of Marisol's pain and just make it disappear.

"Come here," he murmured, reaching for her.

Without having to explain his intentions, she understood. She was surprisingly agile for wearing those fuck-me boots. Within seconds she straddled him, stretching her petite body over his.

Her dress rode up over her legs, pushing up high enough that he could see a peek of bright red panties. His hands settled on her thighs. She tensed under his touch, but her hips rolled once, her own response to him clear. Even with clothes on, he could feel the heat of her rubbing over his cock.

Like a mindless animal, his body wanted to fuck, but the pain he'd sensed from her still lingered in the air. "Tell me what happened to your family," he murmured.

"I can't. Not yet," she whispered. More than anything he wanted to push and force her to tell him, but he didn't have the heart to. Not when he could sense her emotional distress. His wolf clawed at him, telling him to comfort her, not talk.

Her dress was some sort of turtleneck thing so he clasped the bottom hem and lifted it upward. With her legs tightly clasping around him, she rose up and allowed him to pull it over her head. He was a little surprised she didn't protest since they were in his SUV, but he could sense her hunger as strong as his own. The mating pull was beyond intense.

Somehow he managed to get the dress free of her body. When he finally got to view what he'd been craving all morning, his cock jerked against his pants, begging to be set free.

Wearing a lacy cherry-red matching bra and panty set with knee-high boots, she was a wet dream come to life. Everything about her drove him wild. Not wanting to remove her bra completely, he shoved the straps then lace cups down to reveal perfect brown nipples tipping her full, round breasts. She shivered under his gaze, but the pain he'd sensed earlier had subsided.

Now all he felt was her desire. It shined from her eyes in white-hot lust and emanated from her body in potent waves that made him and his wolf a little bit wild. And all he wanted at that moment was to be inside her. He wanted to ease her ache as much as he wanted her to ease his own.

Taking him off guard, she reached down and clasped her fingers around his belt buckle. Her hand slipped once so he took over, unwilling to wait. He hadn't bothered with boxers because he didn't want the extra barrier. He wanted to fuck Marisol when and where he wanted with as little trouble undressing as possible.

When he lifted his hips, she loosened the grip she had with her thighs and helped him tug his pants down. His movements were constrictive and it was surprisingly hot. Normally he liked to be completely in control of everything. He cupped the back of her head before devouring her mouth. Kissing and teasing her tongue in much the same way he'd teased her pussy earlier, he tried to remind himself to give her *some* foreplay, but his cock wasn't listening. He loved the way she tasted, couldn't get enough of it.

She rolled her hips against his, and each time her lace-covered mound rubbed against his dick, he moaned into her mouth.

"You make me crazy, female," he murmured against her.

"Back atcha."

He felt as if his body was on fire and Marisol was the only thing that could douse it.

Dipping his head, he sucked one of her nipples into his mouth. As he traced his tongue around the hardened bud she arched her back, pushing herself deeper into his mouth.

She made tiny gasping sounds as she rubbed her body against his. Her fingers clutched his shoulders tightly and each time he tugged on her nipple, her body trembled.

He continued his assault on her breast and at that moment, he wished he had more hands. He wanted to touch all of her at the same time. His hands trailed up her thighs around to her ass. Smooth, tight skin greeted him. Dipping his finger underneath the stretchy material of her thong, he pulled it back and let it snap against her soft skin.

"Ah," she moaned, her body jolting at the action, and threaded her fingers through his hair.

Even through the lace barrier, he could feel how wet she was. Keeping one finger under the strap of her thong, he trailed back to the front of her body before pushing the flimsy material to the side. He cupped her mound and rubbed his middle finger over her soaking folds without penetrating. When she surged against him he grasped her hips and lifted her so her opening hovered over his cock.

"You ready?" he asked.

Wordlessly, she nodded.

"Say it." Because he fucking needed to hear it, needed to hear her say she wanted him.

"Yes."

"Say you want me in you."

She wiggled against his grip, but he held firm. This was torturing him as much as her. He would hear her say it. "Stephan," she rasped out.

He pushed up slightly, teasing her.

"Damn it, in me now." Her words were a rough growl.

Without pause he surged into her, pushing balls-deep with one long thrust.

"Stephan," she groaned.

He wanted more. He wanted his name on her lips at all times. He wanted her to think of him whenever she touched herself, whenever he couldn't be with her. Thrusting forward, he didn't give her time to adjust as he stretched and filled her.

Her pussy spasmed and tightened around him as he thrust forward again. When she moaned loudly he froze, worried he'd hurt her. At his pause, she lifted up and slammed down onto him again and again. She took him to the hilt and still wanted more.

Mesmerized, he stared at her as she rode him and had to force himself not to come. He was so close, but he wanted to make sure she came first. Her eyes were closed and her dark hair tumbled around her face and shoulders in thick waves.

"Touch yourself," he murmured. He could easily do it, but he was desperate to see her teasing herself.

Without opening her eyes, one of the hands that had been clasping his shoulder so tightly found its way between her legs. He stared at the vision of his cock driving into her sweet body while she rubbed herself.

It was too much to bear. Leaning forward, he kissed her other breast, licking and laving the top and underside before zeroing in on her rock-hard nub. The second his tongue touched it, her inner walls clamped tighter around his erection.

It was as if her pussy was connected to what he was doing with his mouth. Lashing his tongue over her nipple again, he groaned when she began spasming around him.

"Just like that, Stephan," she whispered.

He cupped her breasts, pushing them up and alternating between which nipple he sucked. The more he teased her, the faster she rode him. She abandoned her clit and clutched the seat behind him. Moving up and down, faster and faster, until her back bowed and she cried out his name, gripping him like a vise until her cream flooded over him.

As soon as her climax started, he allowed himself to let go. He released her breasts and gripped her hips. Letting his head fall back against the headrest, he slammed his cock upward into her tight sheath.

His balls pulled up painfully tight, but it was the sweetest pain he'd ever experienced. Looking at her, touching her, being inside her was fucking heaven. He wanted to claim her so badly he could feel his canines start to extend, but he forced them back.

He might be ready but she sure as hell wasn't. With a loud shout, he jerked upward completely emptying himself. Even as he rode through his orgasm, his cock blindly jutted into her until she'd completely sucked him dry.

She didn't attempt to move away from him and for that he was thankful. He tightened his grip around her back, encircling her waist so that she was snug against him. Their labored breathing and the heady scent of sex overpowered the interior cabin. Traces of sadness lingered around her, but so did satisfaction and something else he couldn't quite put his finger on.

They needed to clean up and he had a lot of explaining to do before he left her with his family, but he didn't want to tear himself away from her just yet. And he really didn't want to leave her alone tonight. His job meant a lot to him, but this case paled in comparison to finding out what had caused her so much pain.

He'd give up taking down Perez for her and that thought alone terrified the holy hell out of him.

CHAPTER NINE

Marisol tried to control the anticipation humming through her. She didn't want Stephan's brother to sense what she had planned. It wasn't as if he could read her thoughts, but Stephan had sensed her emotions in the vehicle earlier and she had no doubt his brother, Thomas, was just as astute. Maybe more so.

She was smart enough to realize that Stephan was blinded by his lust enough that he hadn't wanted to push her by asking questions about her family. She'd overheard his conversation earlier with Thomas and she knew her grace period was coming to an end. After tonight he'd no doubt want answers, but it probably wouldn't matter after what she was about to do.

She quickly shoved her cocktail dress, stilettos, phone, gun and purse into her backpack then tossed it out the bedroom window. Thomas had already canvassed the yard once so she crossed her fingers that he wouldn't see her bag lying in the bushes.

Once she'd shut and locked the window, she hurried downstairs. Luckily, she found Thomas in the kitchen. "Hi." She hovered by the doorway, unsure how he'd react to her request.

He nodded politely at her as he pulled a beer from the refrigerator. He had the same muscular build as Stephan. "Hi. Would you like a drink or something?"

She shook her head. "No, uh, I was wondering…would you mind if I went for a quick run along the beach?" He frowned so she rushed on. "I ran with Stephan earlier and he said it's private, right?"

"My family owns most of the houses for miles in each direction."

"I'm just a little worried about Stephan. He obviously couldn't tell me what he was doing tonight, so I thought it would be okay if I just stretched my legs and worked off some of my tension." *Lord, she was rambling and couldn't seem to stop herself.* He was going to say no. She could feel it in her bones.

"All right. Just don't go far."

Surprise bowled her over, but before he could change his mind, she hurried toward the back door. "Thanks. And uh, would you mind not looking while I uh…" Most wolves were unabashed in their nudity, but she didn't relish the thought of Stephan's brother seeing her nude.

He frowned for a moment until understanding dawned on his face. "Oh right. Of course. I'll give you privacy." He cleared his throat and strode from the room.

She rushed out the back door and changed as soon as she'd stripped. The pain rushed over her as her bones cracked and realigned, but the adrenaline pumping through her overrode most of her normal discomfort. She scanned the back of the house just to make sure Thomas wasn't watching through one of the windows—not that she'd actually expected him to—before grabbing her backpack between her teeth and bounding across the yard.

Her time was limited and she had to hurry or her friends wouldn't wait for her.

* * *

Thomas cursed as he glanced at his watch. Marisol had been gone long enough that he knew she wasn't coming back. Something had been off about her scent, but he'd pushed his instinct aside because she was his brother's mate. Stephan had been so damn protective about her; Thomas hadn't wanted to spook or offend her.

He wasn't sure what she was up to, but if she planned to hurt his brother, he'd take care of her himself. He tucked his clothes and cell phone into a small bag before changing.

Picking up her scent wasn't hard. She wore a distinctive jasmine perfume and there was something else about her that was solely hers. Not to mention she had his brother's scent all over her. Being a wolf definitely had advantages.

After trailing her a mile down the beach, her fragrance shifted back toward the mainland, away from the water. According to Stephan, Marisol was a small dog so it would be easier for her to blend in. He, on the other hand, weighed about one hundred twenty-five pounds and he *looked* like a wolf. Whereas some of the others in his pack had softer qualities and looked more like pets, nothing about him was soft. He knew he looked ferocious in his shifted form so he had to be careful.

Sticking to the shadows, he managed to blend in as he raced through neighborhoods. It wasn't late, but the sun had set and most people were in for the evening. The few cats he came across scurried when they saw him.

Her scent started to fade when he spotted her in human form, waving at someone. She stood on a sidewalk in front of a modest sized house. She was half bent over, slipping her foot into a high-heeled shoe. After straightening her dress, she shoved something under a cluster of bushes.

He wanted to change and stop her, but by the time he shifted he wouldn't be able to put clothes on and catch her. Since running naked wasn't an option, he was screwed. Sticking to the shadows, he watched as she got into the backseat of a luxury car and slammed the door. As the car sped away, he ducked behind a cluster of oversized elephant ear leaves and changed. After the pain subsided, he called his brother.

* * *

Marisol fought the guilt coursing through her. She was a complete and total asshole. No doubt about it. Not only had she lied to the man she was falling for, she'd lied to his brother too.

"I'm so glad you wanted to come out tonight. This party is supposed to be amazing." Talia, the tall blonde Marisol had gone out with last night, glanced at her in the rearview mirror from the driver's seat.

Marisol plastered on a big smile. "I wouldn't miss it."

"I can't believe Antonio Perez is actually having a party at his house. I've never been before but I heard the place is absolutely sick. Three stories, a tennis court..."

As Talia and the other two girls in the car droned on, Marisol managed to answer their questions and laugh when appropriate. Still, it was impossible to fight the nausea threatening to overwhelm her. This was supposed to have been easy. All she needed to do was get Perez alone and she'd kill him. One shot. That was all she needed. Then all the guilt and suffering she'd experienced over the past year would go away. Even if she died. Especially if she died. It was her fault her family was dead anyway. Maybe she didn't deserve to walk away after killing Perez. Just a week ago she wouldn't have cared. Now... all she could seem to think about was

Stephan and how this would hurt him. It was the last thing she wanted to do but her pack deserved justice.

When she thought about her family, her skin felt too tight for her body. It was almost impossible to breathe. She actually had to focus on *not* changing. Her thoughts strayed to Stephan and even though her heart rate increased, the desire to change decreased. If she could just keep her attention on him and what they'd shared together, she could control her body. Of course if she did that, she also had to focus on her guilt at lying to her mate, but that was just the price she had to pay.

When they finally pulled down Perez's long, winding driveway, two armed men stopped their car. After checking the trunk, the men waved them through. Marisol had been banking they wouldn't check their purses. If they had she would have been screwed. Or she'd have just explained it away. After all, who was going to hide a gun in a small clutch. Besides, no one was dumb enough to try to kill Perez when he was surrounded by armed guards.

Well, no one but her. It was why she was using a gun and not her shifter strength. It would be easier to get to him this way.

After they'd parked, Talia hooked her arm through Marisol's. "Come on, let's head around back to the pool area."

The other woman was a little flighty, but she was incredibly sweet and Marisol was thankful she'd been willing to pick her up as late as she'd called. Blood rushed in her ears as they walked along the stone path leading to the backyard. Loud music and voices trailed around the palatial monstrosity.

Almost as soon as they rounded the corner, a man carrying a tray of champagne greeted them. Just to keep her hands busy, she took one. Scantily clad women, men in suits and armed guards milled around the backyard. White twinkle lights were strung up around the gazebo and waiters with trays of food and drinks casually mingled with everyone.

Scanning the crowd, her gaze automatically landed on Stephan. With his height and size, he stood out anyway, but now that they'd slept together, she'd be able to pick his scent out anywhere. It was almost as if his scent had grown stronger, been etched in her memory.

As she drank in the sight of him, his head turned and his dark, penetrating eyes locked on hers. He looked at her as if he'd like to swallow her whole. But he didn't look surprised to see her. No, he looked angry, as if he'd been expecting her.

"Shit," she muttered under her breath. Thomas must have called him.

"Oh isn't that Stephan Vasquez?" Talia cooed. "I heard you went home with him last night, naughty girl."

She said something else, but Marisol zoned out as Stephan stalked toward her.

She was on the other side of the yard, but he moved effortlessly through the mix of people. His dark eyes were practically gleaming as they zeroed in on her. When a tall brunette touched his arm, he glanced to his side and Marisol took the opportunity to hide.

Ducking behind Talia, she grabbed her friend's hips and used her as a shield. Talia was slim, but she was tall.

"Oh my God, what the hell are you doing?" Talia laughed.

"Hide me. Let's get inside," she whispered.

Talia giggled loudly but did as she asked. Sidestepping a few people, they hurried toward the back entrance of the house. "I take it you don't want a repeat of last night and he does. Was he bad in bed?" She laughed again, seeming to think the whole situation was hilarious.

Marisol peeked around Talia's lithe form and spotted Stephan talking to the woman who had grabbed his arm. Unwanted jealousy sparked through her like a brush fire, but the fact that he looked annoyed and bored went a long way to soothing her annoyance. Not that she should be focusing on her jealousy anyway.

"We're almost there," Talia muttered under her breath.

Once they ducked into Perez's house, Talia plucked the champagne glass from Marisol's hand. "This is my payment for helping you out. And you better not think you're getting away without telling me what's going on with Mr. tall, dark and dangerous. Come on, spill… was he bad in bed?"

She opened her mouth with a lame excuse when a shriek from a few feet away interrupted them. A girl Marisol vaguely recognized ran up to Talia and embraced her in a drunken hug. She knew it was crappy to abandon her friend, but Marisol skirted through the thick throng of guests until she was able to duck into one of the downstairs bathrooms. It was down one of the hallways and away from the crowd. She hadn't seen anyone come this way so she figured she was safe for a few minutes.

Once inside, she locked the door and dumped the contents of her purse onto the counter. She unfolded the printed layout of Perez's home and pinpointed where she was. Getting this had cost her a lot of money, but it had been worth it. Apparently he'd had an additional room built and a steel door with biometric security installed. She wasn't sure what was behind it, but whatever it was, it was important to him.

Now all she needed to do was find a place to hide and wait for the party to end. Once she got him alone—or relatively alone—she was going to do what she had to.

She re-folded the paper and shoved it and everything else back into her small purse. As she stepped out, ready to ease the door shut behind her, a large hand clamped over her mouth and another hand snaked around her waist, pulling her flush against a strong body.

She started to scream when Stephan's scent slammed into her. Lord, she hadn't even smelled him coming. She'd been too caught up in her plans. Before she could think about struggling, Stephan opened the door and practically toppled over her into the bathroom.

Grasping her by the shoulders he swiveled her around so she was facing him. His fingers bit into her skin through the thin material of her dress. "What the hell are you doing here?" The question was asked calmly, but there a deadly edge to his voice that, while it shouldn't have surprised her, scared the hell out of her.

"I, uh..."

"Don't lie to me, Marisol."

She swallowed at the way he said her name and tried to take a step back. When she did, her butt hit the counter and he simply advanced on her, moving like the lethal predator he was. He leaned forward and placed his hands on the edge of the counter, caging her in and forcing her to arch her back against him. She gasped when she felt his erection pressing against her lower abdomen.

"I'm waiting for an answer." There was a slight rise to the pitch of his voice.

"I..." She couldn't say it. The words refused to come. Nervously, she tried to shift her weight, and when she did, her purse clattered to the floor. She darted a quick glance at it and couldn't help the surge of nerves that skittered through her.

Stephan narrowed his eyes and looked at her purse then at her. Her lungs squeezed as he stared at her. Without giving her a chance to react, he snatched it off the floor and jerked it open.

"What the fuck is this?" he rasped out, his voice deadly quiet. He withdrew her gun and stared at her.

Unable to meet his gaze, she focused on the floor. She couldn't explain it to him and now she'd screwed up her one chance to take down Perez. Not only that; she'd ruined everything with her mate. Her throat seized as she tried to fight the sudden onslaught of tears coming. Oh God, she hadn't cried in forever. She couldn't have a breakdown now. Not here.

A stray tear slipped down her cheek. Before it even reached her chin, Stephan cupped her jaw and tilted her head upward. Anger radiated from him, but his expression was a little softer. And a lot less intimidating. Which was somehow worse. Dealing with his anger seemed like a better option.

"Why do you have a gun?"

She took a deep breath, steadied herself. "I came here to kill Antonio Perez."

Her shallow breathing and the blood rushing in her ears were the only sounds she heard and they seemed to permeate every nook of the otherwise silent room.

The hand that embraced her jaw slid around until he cupped her head in a harsh grasp. It didn't hurt, but it left no room for doubt who dominated the room. He opened his mouth, but a familiar male voice called his name from the hallway.

It was Perez.

Marisol froze, unsure what to do, but Stephan stripped his shirt off then grabbed her by her hips and lifted her onto the counter. She barely had time to blink before he'd spread her thighs wide, forcing her dress up to her waist. She had no choice but to wrap her legs around him.

"I saw him go in here, boss," someone said.

Stephan covered her mouth with his in a possessive claiming. His kisses were harsh and angry and incredibly passionate. As he stroked her tongue with his, her fear gave way to desire. His fingers threaded through her hair on either side of her head so she clutched onto his shoulders. Her panties dampened when he shifted and ran one of his hands up her thigh, trailing under her dress and under the thin material covering her mound.

The sound of the door opening tore them apart.

"Get the fuck out of here!" Stephan barked.

Through a haze, she made out the figure of Perez and someone else, probably one of his bodyguards. The door shut immediately, no doubt because they realized what Stephan was doing.

"Meet me in twenty minutes," Perez shouted through the door.

Stephan grunted a non-answer then resumed his assault on her mouth, but not before locking the door. As his tongue rasped against hers, she moaned and locked her ankles behind his back.

With each stroke of their tongues, his cock surged against her. He pulled his head back and muttered a string of obscene curses that probably shouldn't have turned her on—but kind of did. She was sure he was going to yell at her or haul her out of there, but instead, he grappled with his belt until his pants slid down his legs.

His very muscular legs.

"What are you doing?" she whispered.

"I'm going to fuck you." That deadly edge was back to his voice, but it was laced with something else.

Desire.

Need.

Hunger.

The command of his voice and the man behind that voice caused every muscle in her to pull taut. She started to slide off the counter so she could shimmy out of her panties, but he stopped her.

He covered her mound with his hand and pushed the flimsy material to the side. Without any warning or foreplay, he buried his cock inside her with a hard thrust.

Her inner walls stretched to take him but he didn't give her any time to adjust. He kept his gaze locked on hers as he pulled out of her then slammed into her again.

In and out. In and out.

Her pussy spasmed each time he drove into her. She wanted to look away from his penetrating gaze but she couldn't. His dark eyes seemed to have some sort of hold on her.

While he didn't make a move to take off the rest of her clothes, he palmed one of her breasts through the silky material of her dress. She hadn't worn a bra and the dress was thin. Her nipples were already hard, but they pebbled painfully under his insistent teasing. He tweaked and rubbed her in erotic little strokes. It was as if an imaginary string was attached to her aching nipples and pulsing clit. Each time he touched her, her clit throbbed.

She was so close that even a little more stimulation would push her over the edge. "I'm so close, Stephan," she moaned.

Her words had the opposite effect of what she wanted. He drove into her. Hard. Then he remained buried, balls-deep and refused to move.

She tried to roll her hips against his but he simply grabbed her and held her in place.

"What are you doing?" she rasped.

"Why do you want to kill Perez?" he demanded, his words so low she might not have been able to hear him if she'd been human.

"You want to know *now?*" His cock was buried to the hilt and ripples swelled through her pussy like the after-effects of an earthquake. If he'd just move a little, she could come.

"Tell me," he whispered before leaning forward and grasping her earlobe between his teeth. He pressed lightly and tugged.

His breath was hot against her neck. She arched her back against him, but he remained immobile inside her. Scorching, singing heat radiated from him with unbelievable force. She could actually feel the warmth coming off him it was so potent. "I can't."

He shifted his hips and pulled out of her by a couple inches. She immediately mourned the loss. "Tell me, she-wolf." His voice was still a whisper.

She was so close to climax. Her body hurt. It ached. And she just needed release. And she desperately needed to tell someone her secret. The words were on the tip of her tongue. She wanted to trust Stephan with this.

"Tell me or I walk out of here," he rumbled.

She believed him. "He killed my entire pack and it's my fault. I want him to pay for what he did." The words tore from her chest with a sob.

He tensed for a split second and some foreign emotion rolled off him. She couldn't place what it was, but before she could even think, he pushed into her and he didn't stop.

His thrusts were rough, shaky, and she couldn't catch her breath before an orgasm rocked through her. Her inner walls clenched around him with ferocity as her climax took over. Not wanting to give anyone a show, she bit into his shoulder to keep from crying out. Pleasure emanated out of her every pore as the waves swept through her.

His corded muscles bunched underneath her teeth but he didn't push her away or show pain. Instead, his grip on her hips tightened and his thrusts increased. He moaned low and deep, but he didn't cry out either as he emptied himself into her. Clutching onto her hips, he kept thrusting until he was completely sated.

She pressed her forehead to his bare chest, unwilling to look him in the eye. To her horror, tears started leaking from her eyes. Stupid, stupid tears. She swallowed against the lump in her throat and tried to force herself not to show weakness, but it was no use.

The harder she tried to control herself, the more she cried. She bit her bottom lip so she wouldn't sob, but

Stephan wouldn't let her go. He cupped her face and feathered kisses all over her. Across her jaw, her cheeks, even her nose. The sweeping motion was sweet and unexpected and it wrenched even more tears from her. He was being so kind and she didn't know why.

"Don't cry, *kardia mou*," he murmured over and over.

She wasn't sure what the endearment meant, but every time he said it, her stomach did a strange flip-flop. Swiping at her errant tears, she met his gaze. "Do you hate me?" She didn't even want to ask, wasn't sure she could handle the answer.

His jaw tightened as he shook his head. "Never."

An awkward silence descended on the room and she suddenly realized how exposed she was. Glancing down, her breath caught at the sight they made. He was still buried inside her and both their juices covered her thighs. Her underwear cut into her skin from being shoved to the side.

He must have understood her discomfort because he slowly pulled out of her and began cleaning her. Once he was finished, she tried to adjust her dress but her hands were too shaky. She'd just admitted her darkest secret to him and he hadn't said anything about it.

Thankfully Stephan was still a gentleman. He helped adjust her clothing before hooking an arm around her waist. He opened the door, then when he was sure the hallway was empty, he stepped out into it and dragged her with him.

"What are you doing?" she whispered.

But he didn't answer. As he strode down the hallway she had no choice but to keep pace. Instead of heading back toward the party, he led her down another hallway that emptied into a foyer. Two large faux Corinthian style columns encased a sturdy looking front door.

A few men with guns stood casually by. When they saw Stephan they nodded at him but didn't make a move to stop them as he opened the door. Her breath hitched when she saw the same tinted SUV from the night before. He opened the back door and practically shoved her inside. "You're going back to my place. I'll see you later." He turned toward the window and muttered something in a foreign language to the same driver as the night before. The young wolf responded then rolled the window up, giving them privacy.

Stephan leaned forward and pressed a soft kiss to her lips. Her mouth still tingled from his previous more demanding kisses and the change of pace was unexpected.

"I'll see you later." His voice was hoarse and raspy. Without giving her a chance to respond, he shut the door and the driver pulled away a second later.

Glancing out the back window, she couldn't help the sinking sensation forming in her gut. He didn't seem as angry as he had earlier, but she really didn't know him well enough to make that observation. A shiver snaked down her spine so she wrapped her arms around herself and leaned back against the leather seat.

There wasn't much she could do now other than wait.

CHAPTER TEN

Stephan barely contained the rage flowing through him as he walked back inside Perez's house. He had to play this carefully or he was going to rip the man's throat out and ruin the entire operation. He was used to schooling his features, but the thought that Perez had hurt his mate was about to send him over the edge. It wasn't something she'd have lied about. Stephan might not know the details, but the truth had been written in every line and curve of Marisol's body—and in her pained scent.

The moment he entered the house, Perez, his men and two of Stephan's teammates were waiting for him. "Everything all right?" Perez asked with a smirk on his face.

"It would have been better if someone hadn't interrupted me." His voice was dry.

A lecherous grin spread across Perez's face. "I'm glad you're having a good time, but now it's time to get down to business."

"Agreed."

"I want to talk to you privately." Perez glanced at his personal guards then at Stephan's men before returning his gaze to Stephan. "Just the two of us."

Stephan nodded. "That's acceptable, but if you try to double-cross me, I'll cut your heart out."

Perez cleared his throat, but nodded. "This way."

Stephan fell in step with the other man as they headed for one of the many hallways in Perez's mansion. He kept track of how many turns they made until they stood in front of a steel door that seemed out of place among the oak-paneled pictures and ornate crown molding lining the hallway.

When Perez placed his hand on a biometric scanner, Stephan could feel the energetic charge rolling off the other man. Just what the hell was behind this door that had him so excited?

As they stepped into a laboratory of some sort, Stephan frowned as he scanned the room. When he saw two naked women strapped down behind a glass window, his gut roiled. "I don't deal with slave girls. I thought that much was clear." But he'd sure as hell come back and rescue these females.

Perez snorted. "These aren't whores. They're...werewolves. And I've managed to duplicate their abilities in regular humans. We will be able to create super soldiers."

Stephan's heart rate increased. *Was Perez testing him?* "Is this some kind of fucking joke? Werewolves? I thought you were serious about doing business with me."

"I am! This is why I called you in here alone. Watch." He picked up something that looked like a PDA and pressed a couple buttons. A flat screen against one of the walls flashed on.

The date stamp on the screen was six months ago. It was near dusk, somewhere close to the ocean. What city or state though, he couldn't be sure. Stephan watched as a team of masked, armed men surrounded a barking dog. The dog yapped and growled but someone shot it with something—*a tranquilizer gun.* The light brown and white Akita yelped in pain before it fell on its side. Then it shifted into a naked blonde woman who looked vaguely familiar.

"What the hell?" He tried to act as astonished as he could.

Perez beamed at him proudly. "So far we've only found two females able to undergo our testing. She is one of them."

"How do I know this isn't staged?" Stephan asked.

"They both have too many drugs in their system now. We've already started reducing their dosage. Once you guarantee me the contacts I require, I'll set up a live demonstration in a very controlled setting. It will be for your eyes only, *before* we meet with any of your friends. I don't have a death wish and I wouldn't try to cross or embarrass you. We can both make a lot of money."

The girl on the video cried out as they threw a net over her. Stephan's hands fisted at his side. *Do not change, do not change, do not change.* His wolf was raging pissed, demanding he unleash all his rage on this piece of garbage who'd chained up wolves for monetary gain. "Why does she look familiar?" He needed to keep the other man talking and he desperately needed to keep his mind off the sight of one of his own kind being hunted.

He shrugged dismissively. "She's a model—*was* a model, for some international clothing company."

Stephan tore his gaze away from the screen. "Who's the other woman in there?"

"Her name isn't important. I got her a year ago. She's the only one of her pack to survive."

"Pack?" Stephan asked while imagining himself ripping Perez's head from his body. He'd do it slowly too, make this fucker suffer.

"That's what they call themselves, if you can imagine." He turned his attention back to the screen and pressed another button.

A new video popped up dated two days ago. The setting was in a warehouse. That much was clear. A man wearing camouflage fatigues lifted a two-door car off the ground. "We'll need to conduct longer studies of course, but so far, the results are what we were hoping for. The human we injected is almost a hundred times stronger and his healing capabilities are like nothing the world has ever seen before. I know this must be a shock to you—"

"How did you find out about these...creatures?"

"One of their own kind betrayed them for a lot of money."

Betrayed. Marisol had said it was her fault—no! His mind immediately rejected the thought. She'd been distraught and she'd come here to kill Perez. She couldn't have done it.

Perez continued. "This is why I wanted to do business with you. You have the contacts I need. If you back me and provide introductions, we can make a fortune."

Stephan's lips pulled into a thin line. "How many of your men know about this?"

"The four in the first video and the doctor who created the serum are the only other people who know about this."

"Good. I need a few days to think things over, but this is between you and me. My men will not be privy to anything you've shown me here." Stephan's heart beat erratically and his blood rushed loudly in his ears. The only thing keeping him from changing was the knowledge that he was going to burn Perez's home to the ground. Possibly with Perez in it.

* * *

Stephan braced himself as he entered the beach house. As soon as he stepped inside he was hit with an array of emotions.

Anger, hurt, fear, pain. And he wasn't sure what was coming from whom. A low murmur of voices trailed from the kitchen so he made his way there.

His father, Nick, Thomas and his Uncle Cosmo stood around the center island, deep in conversation. Marisol and his mother sat at the table near one of the windows. Marisol's eyes were red and puffy. The wolf inside him cried out to comfort her, but duty prevented him. He risked a quick glance at his mother. She didn't look necessarily angry, but her dark eyebrows rose questioningly at him.

The men became silent as he entered the room. He could feel Marisol's gaze bore into him but he couldn't look at her again. If he did, he was likely to take her into his arms and drag her upstairs to take care of her. The need to take care of his mate was all-consuming.

"You should have told me you found a mate," his father said.

Stephan nodded at the same time Thomas spoke, "He was going to after he wrapped his case up. A day or two would *not* have made a difference."

As next in line to be Alpha, Thomas had more leeway than any other male in the pack, but Stephan didn't want his brother to stand up for him. Not now. He'd fucked up and he deserved the rebuke. Still, he appreciated his brother's loyalty.

"It doesn't matter. The pack comes first." His father didn't raise his voice because he didn't have to. His command and presence enveloped the entire room. At two-hundred years old, he looked barely forty-five. Standing over six feet, there was no sign of gray in his dark hair and his dark eyes had an unmistakable air of insight—and deadliness.

Stephan knew there would be time enough later to discuss his mistakes. "We have more important problems to worry about." As quickly as he could, he explained everything he'd seen at Perez's house. When he was finished, an eerie silence descended on the kitchen.

His father was the first to speak. He focused on Marisol. "Did you know Perez was doing experiments on shifters?"

Eyes wide, she shook her head. "No, I swear. He killed all the males of our pack and most of the females. I thought… I just thought he hated our kind." The truth was there in the shakiness of her voice.

"What did you tell your boss, Stephan?" This time Thomas spoke.

Stephan paused at his brother's question. Thomas had been looking out of him and Nick since they were pups. It wasn't lost on him that his brother cared about

Stephan's job—something his father didn't concern himself over. "I lied to my team. They think Perez wants time to think about doing business with me. I managed to buy myself a week at the most."

"We cannot wait a week. We'll move against him tonight," his father said.

The others murmured in agreement with the exception of Nick. "We need a plan first. If this guy is experimenting on shifters, he's going to have proper weapons to hurt us. I think half of us should go in human form, the other half, shifted."

His father and the others nodded. That still didn't alleviate the fact that they didn't have the schematics of Perez's house or know how many men they'd be up against, but they'd make it work. Stephan knew the layout of the first floor so that would have to be good enough.

"I might be able to help," Marisol's soft voice silenced the rest of the room. Her hands shook as she opened her small purse. "This is the design plan for Perez's house."

Stephan was across the room before anyone could move. He frowned as he scanned it. The DEA hadn't been able to get this because it hadn't been recorded online anywhere. "How did *you* get this?"

"Luck and money. I met the architect a few months ago at a club in South Beach. It took a lot of sweet talking and cost a small fortune, but he gave me a copy."

He held out his hand to her. She stared at it for a moment before placing her much smaller one in his then stood. Stephan glanced at his family. "Give me a second." He didn't wait for a response as he led her from the kitchen. He kept walking until they were upstairs and out of earshot.

Once they were alone, he placed his hands on her hips and pulled her close. Touching her soothed his wolf on so many levels. "Are you okay?"

She tensed under his touch and shrugged, the action jerky. "Your family is *not* happy with me."

"They'll get over it." Because he wasn't letting this female go.

She swallowed hard. "I don't really care about them...no offense. I just care what you think."

He wasn't exactly happy she'd lied to him either, but that wasn't what she needed to hear. Part of him wanted to shake her senseless, but more than anything he just wanted to take her in his arms and comfort her. "Why didn't you tell me about Perez?"

"I... I didn't think I'd even get out of his house alive. I just needed one shot to kill him and..." Tears rolled down her cheeks as she trailed off.

And she'd been willing to die to do it. The words hung silently in the air. He wasn't sure how to even digest her words. The thought of her willingly going into a situation like that without backup... it sliced him up.

He gently wiped away her tears. "I have to go, but we *are* going to talk about this."

"I know," she whispered.

So many things still needed to be said but time wasn't his friend. They needed to catch Perez unaware. His guard would be down tonight. Stephan had seen the greed in his eyes earlier. Perez was ready to deal and he thought he had a sure thing with Stephan *Vasquez.* He'd made his first big mistake by settling in Miami.

Stephan was going to make damn sure that son of a bitch didn't make it out of his house alive tonight. Then he was going to hunt down whoever had betrayed Marisol's pack.

CHAPTER ELEVEN

In wolf form, Stephan edged along the perimeter of Perez's expansive backyard. He'd already knocked out two armed guards using brute strength. Thomas, his father and he had opted to shift because they were stronger in wolf form and looked a hell of a lot more intimidating than the other two who'd stayed in human form. Using the overgrown foliage and gazebo as cover, he blended in with the shadows.

The males of his pack had spread out and they were converging on the house from all angles. It would give them the element of surprise.

With his heightened senses, everything around him was clearer. In addition to the men he'd knocked out, a guard or someone not of his pack was nearby. He could smell the individual. Tobacco and a specific body odor accosted Stephan's senses. As he peered around one of the bushes, he spotted a man sitting on one of the lounge chairs by the pool smoking a cigarette.

Stephan could sense other bodies, but he couldn't make out anyone else that was closer than the lone guard. He hoped his brothers had already immobilized the outside guards.

Crouching as low as he could, he inched toward the outside stone fireplace that sat between him and the guard. He just wanted to stun the guy, not kill him, so he had to be careful.

After the guy tossed his cigarette to the ground and stepped on it, he bent to pick up his M4. In that moment, Stephan made his move.

Using all his momentum and strength, he pounced from his hiding position and tackled him from behind. His paws slammed into the man's back. The guy let out a shout as they tumbled over the chair, but his head struck the stone tile and his entire body stilled. Which was exactly what Stephan had hoped for. Fighting for even minutes wasn't in the game plan. They needed to immobilize these men and take the house.

Stephan nudged him with his paw, but the man didn't move.

"He's out cold," Nick murmured as he bent next to the man and secured his wrists behind his back. He tapped his ear. "Cosmo says it's clear out front and I took out three other armed men. I guarantee Thomas and Dad have taken out more."

Stephan understood his brother, but he couldn't respond. In shifted form, he could project thoughts with his mind, but his brother would only understand him if he was in wolf form too.

As they continued toward the back patio, Thomas rounded the corner. Once they were all together by the French doors, Thomas ordered him to shift to human form.

Pain rippled through Stephan until he was on his knees and groaning. Changing back to human form always hurt worse.

Nick had already pulled most of their clothing from his backpack by the time he and Thomas had changed. Wordlessly, they slipped on black fatigues and long-sleeved black shirts. With the weapons they'd brought, there hadn't been enough room to include shoes.

"Dad and Cosmo are going in through the front," Thomas whispered.

The back door was locked so instead of wasting time picking it, Stephan broke the glass and unlocked it manually. A piercing alarm sounded as they rushed inside. Before leaving their family's beach house, they'd all studied the layout of Perez's house. Everything on the diagram corresponded with the layout he remembered from his short visit.

Now they simply needed to make it to the lab and figure out a way to get inside before any cops showed up.

"We've got two minutes," Thomas shouted above the noise.

As they fanned out across the open living room, two guards appeared from around the corner. Both men raised their pistols.

Stephan fired at the one on the right. The man fell at the same time his partner did. Either Thomas or Nick had taken him down with one shot. It had been decades since he'd been in an all-out gunfight, but the last time had been with his brothers in Vietnam. After almost two-hundred years of living and fighting together, it was only natural they knew how to work as a team.

Sidestepping the fallen men, Stephan crouched low then rounded the corner. The hallway was empty so he motioned to his brothers. As werewolves, regular bullets wouldn't kill them but they would still cause excruciating pain.

When they neared the end of the hallway a loud explosion ripped through the air so Stephan and his brother picked up their pace. They rounded the corner and into the hallway leading toward the laboratory.

Stephan nearly stumbled at the sight in front of them.

"What the hell?" Nick shouted above the alarm.

The steel door leading to the lab was blown off and smoke billowed out from the room. As they neared the door, the petite brunette he'd seen strapped down appeared in the open entrance.

She was completely naked but a bright blue ball of—something, maybe energy or lightning—crackled in her hands. She lifted a hand as if to fire at them but paused as she smelled the air. As she looked at the three of them, it was as if all the energy was sucked from her body. Her eyes rolled back in her head and she collapsed in a small, lifeless heap.

"I'll grab the girl. Torch the lab!" Thomas said as he sprinted ahead of them. He scooped her up as Stephan and Nick headed inside.

Glass shards covered most of the tiled floor, the television screen was cracked and the beakers and test-tubes he'd seen earlier were smashed on the floor. Three guards and an old man in a lab coat lay dead on the floor with giant holes burned through their chests. What had once been a two-way mirror was now shattered open. Stephan spotted the blonde woman huddled in a corner. She was naked and dirty, but her eyes were open and terrified.

"I got her." Nick tossed the bottle of lighter fluid to Stephan before bounding over the glass. His boots made crunching sounds, even above the siren.

As Stephan started spraying everything with the accelerant, his father and uncle ran into the room, both in human form.

"Everyone is down but Perez isn't here." His father flipped open his silver lighter and tossed it into the middle of the room.

Flames erupted with a loud whoosh. Bright orange fire licked its way across the floor, eating everything in its path with a hungry intensity. Stephan had wanted to gather some sort of records, but there was no time.

The cops—or worse, the DEA—would be arriving soon and Stephan knew he couldn't be anywhere around.

They all rushed from the room and sprinted back the way they'd come. An explosion ripped through the house, rocking the foundation, as they emptied onto the back patio.

The familiar blare of a fire truck siren screamed through the night.

"Shift!" his father ordered.

Regardless of their state of dress, they all changed. Thomas and Nick were already long gone with the women.

If they wanted to get away from the cops, they couldn't be in human form. Stephan stayed close to his father and uncle as they ran across the backyard. Shouting humans sounded around them, but no one tried to stop them and Stephan didn't pause to see who had arrived. Considering the growing fire and the potential problem that caused, a couple of loose dogs roaming around wouldn't even register on Miami PD's radar in a situation like this.

The farther they ran, the more his paw ached. A piece of glass must have embedded itself in his foot, but that was the least of his worries. When his father slowed, so did Stephan and his uncle. They neared the quiet dead-end road where his father had left his SUV.

Luckily, the back hatch was open and Nick stood guard. The three of them dove inside and Nick slammed the door shut behind them. Moments later, the vehicle jerked to life. Only then did Stephan allow himself to think about what they'd just done. Everything had happened so quickly and they hadn't had adequate time to cover their tracks. If they made just one slip-up, it could send their entire pack on the run and into hiding.

CHAPTER TWELVE

Marisol's eyes flew open at the sound of familiar voices. She pushed the afghan throw off and rubbed her eyes. She and Stephan's mother must have fallen asleep in the living room. Glancing around, she groaned when she saw the clock on the mantle. *Four o'clock.*

"They're here," Alisha murmured as she pushed up from the loveseat.

Stephan's mother had been strangely quiet since the males of the Lazos pack had left hours before. Of course she hadn't let Marisol out of her sight, but she also hadn't drilled her with questions.

Footsteps across the tiled entryway and the front door slamming jerked Marisol out of her daze and into action. In addition to all the familiar bodies she scented something else. Something—*someone*—very familiar. But it couldn't be. Hope bloomed inside her, so sharp she was afraid to believe what she scented.

She hurried out of the room and almost ran directly into Stephan. He wore tattered shorts and no shirt or shoes. She instantly reached for him, wanting to comfort him. "Are you okay?"

He stepped back and kept about a foot of distance between them. "We're fine. The lab is destroyed and probably Perez's entire house."

"What about Perez?" Marisol was vaguely aware as Alisha passed them and headed toward the kitchen. Her heart hurt at Stephan's rejection so she wrapped her arms around herself.

"We didn't find him, but there were two survivors. Both female werewolves. He's been experimenting on them, but they seem physically fine. One of them is different..."

Instinctively she tensed at his guarded tone. Maybe what she'd scented was real after all. "What do you mean?"

"I'm not sure. Most of the lab was destroyed when we got there. One of the she-wolves we saved harnessed some sort of blue light in her hands."

"Blue?" Marisol's heart skipped a beat. Oh God, could it be her?

"Yes, almost like lightning—"

Marisol sidestepped him and raced for the kitchen. Her bare feet smacked against the cool tile. She tried to control the hope that surged through her, but it was useless. As she entered the kitchen, that hope blossomed with the intensity of a hurricane.

"Paz!" Her sister's limp form was stretched out on the center island of the kitchen, covered by a large towel.

Thomas stood next to her sister, wiping soot and dirt from her face, but she ignored him as she took Paz's hand.

It was warm. A good sign. If her sister used too much of her powers, she drained herself of energy. But she was alive. That was all that mattered.

"You know her?" Stephan's voice sounded close behind her.

"Paz, she's my sister. I thought… I thought she was dead." Something in the back of Marisol's mind taunted her that this was a dream, but in her heart she knew it wasn't. Clasping her sister's hand, she breathed a sigh of relief when Paz's fingers tightened slightly.

Experience told her it would be hours before Paz woke up, but Marisol didn't care.

"What is she?" Stephan asked.

Mindless of everyone's gaze on her, she focused on Stephan. She could lie and tell him she didn't know what he meant. Of course if she did, everyone in the room would know she was a liar and she was tired of lying to him anyway. "She's half werewolf, half-fae."

"Faerie?" Alisha gasped from the other side of the room.

Marisol nodded and tried to force down the burst of fear that bloomed in her chest. Stephan was her mate. He wouldn't harm her or her family. Or at least she hoped he wouldn't. Technically Paz was more powerful than everyone in this room—the Alpha included—but she was passed out and helpless. "Her mother was full-blooded faerie, but she wasn't evil, like the Council seems to think faeries are. My father and her mother fell in love, but Selena—that was her mother—died giving birth to Paz. Decades after her mother died, he met and mated with my mother. My father never told the Council about her and the entire pack was sworn to secrecy because..." Marisol swallowed and glanced away from the penetrating gazes of the Lazos pack.

She didn't need to say it aloud because they would understand. The Council of Werewolves would have ordered Paz to die simply because of the magic that ran through her blood. The Cabrera pack wouldn't have listened and it would have begun a bloody war. Millennia ago—long before any of them had been born—faeries and werewolves had been at war. Of course, werewolves had also been at war with vampires, Immortals and any other being that was different. Their history was just as violent as the humans.

"What are her powers?" Lucas asked. His voice was calm, but it didn't stop a tremor of fear from snaking down Marisol's spine.

She risked a quick glance at Stephan. His face was an unreadable mask, but at least he stood by her side. That felt like something. "She...she has the ability to draw energy—life force, I guess you'd call it—from most living beings. It usually manifests in the form of blue light. Basically she turns kinetic energy into a blast of power…it looks sort of like lightning. She's never killed anyone though and from the time she was a child our father helped her to control her powers."

"She killed the men in the lab." Lucas's voice was wry.

"Then they deserved it!" Even though Lucas was an Alpha, she couldn't stop the rising pitch of her voice. She would die for her sister if need be.

Lucas nodded once. "They certainly did. For now, your sister is under the protection of my pack. However, no one outside of this room will know that she's more than a werewolf."

Relief flooded Marisol's veins until her gaze fell on a tall blonde woman leaning against one of the counters. A black t-shirt fell to mid-thigh, but she was dirty and otherwise naked. "Who are you?"

The blonde cast a nervous glance at Lucas, who simply nodded. The she-wolf wrapped her arms around herself defensively. "My name's Shea Hart. I've been held captive with your sister for about six months. She kept me sane and she saved my life. I won't tell a soul about her. I swear it. I owe her so much…" she trailed off with a broken whisper.

The truth of the woman's words rolled over her along with a healthy dose of grief and sadness. Marisol could only imagine what the pretty blonde had been through. Apparently the woman's emotions hit the other wolves in the room too because Lucas immediately took charge.

"Shea, you're coming home with Alisha and me. Stephan, I'm sending over Caro to look at your mate's sister. Everyone else, go home, get a few hours of sleep, we meet at my house at noon." He turned his dark gaze to Marisol. "If your sister is awake, she comes too."

Without a word, Marisol nodded as everyone filed out. She noted that Thomas lingered by Paz, but he eventually made his way toward the door. Once everyone had gone, Marisol made a move toward Stephan but he averted his gaze. "I'll carry your sister upstairs. My aunt should be here soon."

Before she could respond, he'd scooped Paz's small body in his arms and strode from the room. Marisol had hoped his annoyance with her would wane with time, but evidently not. Sighing, she followed him up the stairs but stopped in their room first. And since when did she start thinking of it as *their* room anyway? Rolling her eyes at herself, she grabbed one of her favorite pajama sets and hurried to the guestroom.

She found Stephan tucking the comforter around Paz. Her heart warmed at the sight. As a werewolf, Marisol was more uncomfortable than most with her nudity, but Paz would die if she knew others had seen her naked. For a half-fae, she was incredibly insecure.

Maybe because she'd grown up feeling like an outsider. It was ironic that considering how powerful she was, Paz had more human attributes than anyone Marisol knew.

"Thank you," she murmured.

He grunted one of his non-responses and disappeared from the room. It took some work, but Marisol dressed Paz in the silk pajamas and tucked her back in. By the time she was finishing, an older female wolf carrying a black bag appeared in the doorway.

"Hi, you must be Marisol. I'm Caro, Alisha's sister." The tall, dark-haired woman waited by the door until Marisol nodded for her to enter.

"Thank you for coming. This has happened to her before and I'm sure she'll be fine." Or Marisol desperately hoped so. She wasn't sure if Paz had drugs or something in her system. "Are you a doctor?"

Caro nodded. "For the better part of this century. I spoke to the other rescued werewolf, Shea. She told me they weren't sexually assaulted, but when your sister is awake, I'm going to speak to her about it."

"Okay." Marisol sat on the bed next to Paz and held her sister's hand as Caro examined her. She was thankful the woman was being so gentle.

After a few minutes, the pretty werewolf stood. "You're right. She's sleeping, but she's okay."

On one level, Marisol had already known that, but hearing someone else repeat the sentiment gave her peace of mind. She stared at the other wolf expectantly and when she didn't make a move to leave, Marisol frowned. "Did you need something else?"

"I'd like to stay and keep an eye on her if you don't mind. You can go sleep with your mate. I'll make sure your sister is safe." It wasn't a request.

Marisol's eyes narrowed. "Did Stephan's father put you up to this?"

She shrugged. "More or less."

Marisol wanted to argue with her. Every fiber in her being wanted to throw a tantrum and insist on staying by Paz's side, but she knew when to pick her battles. Her sister was passed out for at least a few hours and this wolf wasn't threatening to her. Besides, she desperately needed to talk to her mate. "If she wakes up, you'll get me?"

The woman nodded. "Of course."

"Immediately?"

A ghost of a smile touched her lips. "Yes."

She placed a quick kiss on her sister's forehead before searching for Stephan. When she entered the bedroom they'd been using, she found the main lights off and he was lying on his side, with his back turned to her. A twinge of pain sliced through her chest, but she knew she deserved his anger. She'd done nothing but lie to him since they'd met.

If she had to go back and do things over, she wasn't sure she'd tell him the truth though. Sighing, she slipped under the sheet and comforter and closed her eyes. She had hoped they'd be able to talk, but it didn't appear he wanted to.

"So that's it?" Stephan's voice cut through the quiet room.

Her eyes flew open. "Is what 'it'?"

"You're just going to go to sleep?"

She sat up in bed. "Do you want to talk?"

The sheets rustled beneath him as he turned to face her. The light from the bathroom streamed in, letting her see the harsh lines of his face.

When he didn't continue, she clutched the sheet tightly in her hands. "I wanted to thank you earlier. I can never repay you for saving my sister...it seems lame to just say thank you, but it's all I can offer."

He sat up fully. "Why did you lie to me?"

"I wasn't sure if I could trust you." It pained her to admit it out loud.

"I told you who I was, what I did for a living."

She bit her bottom lip. "I know, I just... I don't know. I thought if I told you I was going to kill Perez you would stop me."

"Damn right I would have stopped you!" He cleared his throat and his tone softened as he continued. "How's your sister?"

"She must have used a lot of energy, but she'll be fine. This has happened to her before... Is your father going to tell the Council?"

"We'll find out for sure in a few hours, but I think I can safely say no. You're my mate; he won't do anything to betray family."

She sighed and collapsed against the pillow. Her sister was alive and safe for now. Just knowing Paz was still alive dulled the desire to kill Perez.

Stephan stayed sitting and stared at her, far too many emotions in his watchful eyes. She shifted under his intense gaze. "What do you want to ask?"

"You said it was your fault your pack died. Did you betray them?"

"No!" She jolted upright, unable to believe he could ask that. "I made a stupid decision, but I would never betray them. *Never.*"

He reached out and took both her hands in his. She tried to tug away, but he was relentless and the truth was, she needed his support.

"Tell me what happened."

"I was stupid. So, so stupid. I met a lone wolf, Preston Morales, and invited him into our pack. I was..." She cleared her throat, wondering how she was going to tell

Stephan this. Mates could get really jealous and territorial and she certainly wouldn't want to hear about him being interested with another female.

"You were involved with him?" he prodded.

"Not physically, but I was attracted to him and I was thinking about sleeping with him. He was charming and good looking and it had been so long since I'd been with a man who—"

"I get it," Stephan cut in.

"Uh, sorry, I'm just trying to explain the history of what happened. I don't know exactly how he did it, but he poisoned the males of our pack and most of the females. He kidnapped me—apparently he wanted to keep me alive—but I escaped. By the time I made it back to my pack's estate, everyone was dead or missing. For months I searched for the missing, but it was useless. After a while, I assumed everyone was dead."

"How did you find out about the connection between him and Perez?"

"I hired an investigator to tear apart Preston's life. That led me directly to Antonio Perez. I found out that my pack's death wasn't the first. It wasn't like I knew for sure, but Perez and Preston were connected all over the states. Each time they did business, werewolves turned up dead or just disappeared. The Doyle pack in northern New York, the Harrington Pack in Montana, and I'm assuming that Shea's pack was killed or she was kidnapped."

"Kidnapped."

She nodded and continued. "When Perez settled in Miami, it appeared he was going to stay for a while. There hasn't been a sign of Preston anywhere so I've just been waiting to make my move...until you came along."

Stephan dropped her hands and scrubbed a hand over his face. "Why didn't you go to the Council?"

"I was scared and to be honest, I didn't want their help. My sister has had to hide who she is her entire life because of them." She had a lot of anger stored up for the Council.

"Fair enough," he muttered.

She could actually feel his anger dissipate and in that instant, she simply wanted to make things right between them. "I never wanted to lie to you, Stephan." She gently cupped his face. His jaw tightened under her touch, but he didn't back away.

Her inner wolf let out a sigh of relief, right along with her human side. They could make things work, she was sure of it.

CHAPTER THIRTEEN

The little vixen had him tied up in knots. He wanted to be angry with her, but he couldn't find enough energy to hold onto it. Not when she looked so dejected and tired…and lost.

When she touched him, he felt the touch all the way to his groin. Need burned deep in his belly, but after the way he'd roughly taken her in the bathroom at Perez's house, he wanted to wait until they made love again.

He was embarrassed at the way he'd lost control. He'd just started fucking her like an animal. She might have come, but it didn't matter. She deserved better than that. "You need to get some sleep." The words tore from his chest, but he had to take care of his mate.

"I don't want to sleep." The dark circles under her eyes told a different story.

"Don't argue." He lay back against his pillow and tugged her with him so that her head was against his chest. Barely seconds passed before her body stilled and her breathing was steady.

"Marisol," he murmured.

She didn't move.

He tightened his grip on her and savored her sweet, jasmine scent. His cock was painfully aware of the sexy woman in his arms and he was slightly pissed because he couldn't do a damn thing about it.

Even if they were mates, they'd started sleeping together before they'd gotten to know one another. If he could go back in time and do things differently, he wondered if he would. Hell, if he *could*.

Just being near Marisol and his normally tight control loosened. Sighing, he closed his eyes and tried to think of anything but her lean body pressed up against his.

* * *

Stephan's eyes flew open as a scream pierced the air. Instinctively he reached out to protect Marisol. She jolted upright at the same time he did but didn't push him away.

"My sister," she said, terror lacing her voice.

They both jumped off the bed, but he placed himself in front of her as they entered the guestroom. His aunt Caro was trying to calm Marisol's sister down, but the small woman had backed up against the headboard and was clutching a pillow in front of her body in self-defense.

When her gaze fell on Marisol, she dropped the pillow. "Marisol? Where am I?"

"You're safe. This is my mate's house. His pack is going to protect us." Marisol hurried to the bed and sat next to her sister.

Stephan's heart squeezed at the way she said mate without hesitation. Her sister glanced over Marisol's shoulder and looked at him. "I remember you."

"I was at Perez's house the night you escaped. We came to rescue you."

"Where's Shea?" Her voice rose as she asked the question.

"She's safe at my parent's house," he said.

Paz let out a sigh of relief. "Good... What about that bastard, Perez?"

"We don't know where he is...yet. But we're going to find him."

"Not if I find him first," Paz muttered.

"How did you escape your bonds?" He knew he should probably wait to grill her, but his father was going to have questions later. If something could help them to find Perez, they needed to know now.

"I built up an immunity to his drugs."

Marisol cleared her throat and glanced back and forth between them. "Stephan, can I talk to my sister alone?"

"Of course." He glanced at his aunt who silently walked out of the room. As he shut the door behind him, the sound of his cell phone ringing made him hurry to his room.

When he saw his boss's number on caller ID, he instantly tensed. "Yeah?"

"Hey, you okay?"

"Yeah, why?"

"I guess you haven't heard. Perez's house was torched sometime early this morning and his body was found mutilated in an abandoned warehouse. Whoever killed him did a real number on his face. It looks like an animal ripped him apart."

"Shit." Stephan didn't have to feign surprise.

"Since I know you're not at the cover house, I want you to stay wherever you are. Lay low for a few days."

"What?"

"I don't know what's going on or if your cover's been blown. You need to stay out of sight. I've already got the rest of the team doing the same thing. Keep your phone close to you. I've also got an outside team investigating Perez's death. As soon as I'm convinced it's safe, I'll bring you and everyone else back in."

"All right, boss." Under normal circumstances he would've fought his boss to come to work, but right now, he needed the down time with his pack and his mate. They needed to regroup and now they needed to figure out who had killed Perez. It wasn't any of them. Of that, he was positive. That left a lot of questions.

When they disconnected, he started to head back to check on Marisol but changed his mind. After a quick shower and shave, he figured he'd given them enough time alone. It was close to noon and he needed answers from her sister before they headed to his parents' house.

As he started to knock, the bedroom door swung open. Marisol nearly stumbled when she saw him.

"I was just coming to find you." She sounded nervous and out of breath.

"We need to leave soon."

"I know she's awake but… I was thinking Paz doesn't need to come. She's been through a lot and she needs to rest. Meeting the whole pack now will be too much. Especially since they know…what she is."

"Okay." The word was out before he could stop himself.

The megawatt smile Marisol gave him was completely worth the anger he might incur from his father. It lit up her face and eyes. Before he realized what she meant to do, she threw her arms around his neck and held tight.

"Thank you," she whispered in his ear.

Her breath tickled his skin, sending unwanted desire shooting through him. He was an idiot. His Alpha had given him a direct order, but if it made his mate happy, he'd sell his fucking soul. Yeah, he was totally screwed where this female was concerned.

She pulled back and glanced over her shoulder at her sister. “There’s food in the kitchen. Hopefully we won’t be gone long.”

Paz stood near the edge of the bed clutching a pair of jeans and a sweater—no doubt clothes from Marisol. “Thanks. And Stephan, thank you…for everything. I promise to meet with your Alpha in a couple days. I just need some time to adjust.”

He nodded and pulled the door shut behind them. “They’re going to have a lot of questions, Marisol.”

“I know. I’m ready to answer all of them. I just can’t believe my sister’s alive. That monster’s been holding her for a year. She thought all of us were dead too.”

“Your sister can sleep easier because Perez is dead.”

“What?” She jerked to a halt in the middle of the hallway.

“I got a call from my boss this morning. He was found dead in an abandoned warehouse.”

“Who killed him?”

“Don’t know yet.” But he planned to find out.

“Wow.” Marisol shook her head as they entered their bedroom.

“What?”

“It feels sort of anticlimactic. I’ve been hunting him for the better part of the year. I expected to feel, I don’t know, different. Now that I have my sister back…” She shrugged and pulled her pajama top off.

He forgot to breathe for a moment as she started to strip out of the rest of her clothes. Braless and wearing only a skimpy thong, she knelt in front of her suitcase and started rummaging through her things.

Stephan sat against the edge of the bed and drank in the sight of her. Even though she was a werewolf, he'd noticed her apprehension at getting naked in front of him before. Now it seemed she had no such hang-ups. His cock jerked when she shimmied into a pair of jeans. There was nothing intentionally sexual about what she was doing, but his body tingled with excitement as he watched her. This was his mate.

His.

When she pulled a black bra from her clothes, he stopped her. "Don't wear a bra."

Her eyes widened. "What?"

"Please," he rasped. He loved the thought of her wearing nothing under her top. Loved knowing he could slide his hand right under her shirt and touch flesh.

A small smile pulled at the corners of her lips. "Okay." She let the bra slip from her fingers, but instead of putting on the sweater she clutched in her other hand, she dropped it too.

Her hips swayed seductively as she walked toward him. He still sat on the bed so she positioned herself in between his open legs. Wrapping her arms around his neck, she leaned forward and pressed her breasts against his chest. He could feel her hardened nipples through the fabric of his shirt.

Groaning, he grasped her hips. "We don't have time," he murmured.

"I know. I just want you to know how grateful I am for everything you've done. I've lied to you at every turn and that's not who I am. I know we're mates, but I want to get to know the real *you* and I don't want to hold anything back from you anymore."

Relief coursed through him at her words. "I can live with that."

"I'm not sure how to say this, but I want to bond with you," she said quietly.

Her calm declaration punched through him. He wanted to bond with her too. He'd been aching to claim her as his own from the moment they'd met. But..."I don't want your gratitude."

Her full lips pulled into a thin line. "This isn't about that."

Another thought formed in his mind. "Are you saying this because you think my pack won't protect your sister otherwise?"

"No!" Her grip around his neck tightened. "I want this. There's a lot we don't know about each other, but if I'd actually had a choice in my mate, I couldn't have picked anyone better. I *want* to be with you."

He leaned forward so that their faces were inches apart. "Once we do this, there's no going back."

The pupils of her eyes widened as she nodded. "I know."

He pressed a light kiss to her lips but released her hips. "Get dressed or we're never going to make it to the meeting." His words were hoarse and uncontrolled.

Grinning, she stepped away from him and tugged the black sweater over her head. Disappointment rushed through him when the sight of her perfectly rounded breasts and light brown nipples disappeared under her clothing, but the rational part of his brain knew it was for the best.

He needed to call his father and tell him everything he knew *before* the meeting. It would go a long way in calming his father's annoyance at Paz's absence.

* * *

Stephan settled into his chair around the table in his father's study. Normally he sat next to one of his brothers, but Nick had given up his seat for Marisol. She darted a nervous glance at him as his father entered the room. Everyone else had already taken their seats around the table and a few hovered near the built-in bookcase. The she-wolf, Shea, was one of the ones that hovered. She obviously felt as uncomfortable as his mate. Not that he blamed either one of them. While he wasn't sure what his Alpha planned, he knew his father would take care of her too. He and his father didn't always see eye to eye on things, but he was a fair leader.

His father glanced in their direction and frowned, no doubt because Paz wasn't with them, but at least he didn't comment. Instead, he took his seat at the round table. "I hope everyone was able to get a few hours of sleep. We have a lot of things to discuss, but I'd like to keep it brief. First things first, my son's new mate has informed me that Preston Morales is the name of the wolf who betrayed her pack. I've contacted the Council and they're already aware of Morales' existence. He's been on their radar for the past couple years but they haven't been able to hunt him down. They didn't realize he had anything to do with taking out the Cabrera pack, but now that they're aware, he's moved to the top of their priority list. Even though he's being tracked, if anyone hears anything from friends—shifter or human—it doesn't matter how unimportant the detail might seem, come to me immediately."

A low murmur of agreement rippled through the room.

His father waited until everyone quieted. "Second, Antonio Perez is dead. I don't think I need to ask, but did anyone have a hand in that?"

The room was silent.

When no one responded, his father continued. "I didn't think so. My sons and I will be investigating his death, but if you hear anything, you come to me first. This leads me to the most important thing. According to Stephan, before Perez died he injected a human male with some sort of serum derived from werewolf blood that gave him super human strength. Everything in Perez's lab, including the doctor doing the experiments, was destroyed, so we don't know who the human is, where he's gone, or even what the exact effects are of the drug he was given. Keep your ears low to the ground for any strange activity here in Miami or elsewhere. The Council is aware of what happened and if this man is discovered, it could send us all into hiding. Before I turn the floor over to Thomas, there is one more thing. Shea Hart and Paz Cabrera are officially under our pack's protection. Until we get them set up with jobs and a living arrangement, they'll be staying at the spare beach house."

Stephan could feel Marisol tense next to him. He cleared his throat, drawing his father's attention in his direction.

His father tilted his head slightly. "Yes?"

"I'd like Paz to stay with Marisol and me." He didn't need to give a reason or excuse. His father should understand why. His mate had been alone for a year. It might cramp his needs a little, but he couldn't take her away from the only family she had left.

"That's acceptable. If Shea is uncomfortable living alone, we'll work something else out." His father glanced at his oldest brother and gave a brief nod.

Next to Stephan, Marisol reached under the table and grabbed his hand. She threaded her fingers through his and squeezed. The show of simple affection wasn't something he was used to, but he squeezed back. In fact, he couldn't remember a time he'd ever held hands with someone. It was a small thing, but it made something warm and foreign swell in his chest.

Truth be told, he hadn't technically dated in the past hundred or so years. When he found a willing female, they carried on a sexual relationship until one tired of the other. Not that he'd actually had that sort of arrangement in a long time. Growing up, he knew what his parents had was special. He'd never wanted to invest too much time with anyone when he knew it wouldn't last.

As Thomas stood, the room seemed to grow even quieter. His father rarely yielded the floor to anyone. Whatever his brother had to say was no doubt important.

"We're going to make a formal announcement to the entire pack, but for now, everyone in this room needs to be aware that Adam Tucker will be arriving in a week. The Council thought it prudent to send him here until

Morales is caught and until we figure out who the infected human is."

A small wave of fear vibrated across the room and even Marisol shifted in her seat next to Stephan. Adam Tucker was the Council's enforcer, for lack of a better word. Whenever there was a problem with any pack, they sent him to keep things in line. Stephan had met the lone wolf once or twice, and on a personal level, he really liked the guy. Still, he understood the fear of everyone in the room. He was at least two hundred fifty years old—yet looked about forty-five—he had no pack to speak of, and when he came to town, werewolves often died.

"He's not coming here to cause trouble for our pack. The Council wants an independent assessment of the situation. If anyone has a problem, don't cross him. Come to your Alpha or me. Any questions?"

No one said a word. Probably because their Alpha and his second-in-command had just laid out a lot to digest. For so many years, they'd lived peacefully all over the globe. Dealing with outsiders wasn't something their pack was used to.

Times were changing and they'd just have to deal.

"Good. Enjoy the rest of your Sunday everyone." When Carly loudly cleared her throat, Thomas stopped everyone. "Don't forget, Nick's birthday is Wednesday and Carly will have everyone's hide if you don't RSVP to her invitations."

His last minute announcement broke the tension in the room. As the meeting broke up, everyone broke off into different conversations. Carly and his mom immediately pounced on Marisol, so he took the time to speak to his brothers and father privately. They convened in the far corner of the huge study.

"Is this serious? The enforcer coming?" Stephan asked. He'd spoken to his Alpha before the meeting but he hadn't mentioned anything about Tucker visiting.

Thomas shook his head. "It's serious but not for us. We have nothing to hide and once he sees that, he'll focus on what he came here to do."

"So when are you bonding with your mate?" His father effectively changed the subject.

Stephan was rarely embarrassed about anything, but even discussing his bonding brought out every protective instinct inside him. What went on between him and Marisol was their business. "Soon...tonight, most likely."

"Good. I'll introduce her to everyone at Nick's birthday." He glanced over his shoulder then nodded at the three of them. "I'm going to take your mother and Shea home, but I want to see the three of you tomorrow after breakfast. We have a lot to discuss."

Once he walked away, Nick spoke. "This is insane. First that crap with the Immortal, now this."

Thomas shook his head. "Go home to your mates, have a lot of sex and get this shit out of your system. If the rest of the pack senses fear from *any* of us, they'll worry. Besides, we've got each other. No one fucks with the Lazos brothers."

Stephan couldn't help but chuckle at that. "You're right about that."

After Nick walked away, Thomas briefly clamped Stephan on the shoulder. "How's your mate holding up?"

"Now that she has her sister back, she'll be fine." He loved his brother, but he didn't feel like divulging anything else about his mate. She hadn't said it outright, but he knew she was worried enough about her privacy and he didn't want to discuss her without her being there.

"I didn't want to say anything in front of the pack, but when Tucker arrives, we'll make it a point to keep Marisol's sister away from him."

Potent relief slid through his veins. "Thank you."

Stephan glanced at Marisol who was deep in conversation with Carly and Nick and grinned. Carly might be human, but she fit right in with their pack and if anyone could bring Marisol out of her shell, it was the tall redhead.

Marisol turned and when their gazes locked, fire and need erupted in a flash. He muttered something to his brother and strode toward her. If he didn't get her home soon, he was going to behave like the animal he was.

CHAPTER FOURTEEN

Marisol's heart rate had increased since the meeting and it hadn't stopped now that they were back at the beach house. She was finally going to bond with her mate. Maybe not this instant, but it was going to happen very soon. Considering the heated looks he'd been throwing her, she guessed tonight. Equal doses of excitement and nerves flowed through her.

After Stephan's declaration that Paz could live with them, she'd had no doubt in her mind that he was the wolf for her. He understood how important family was. That much was obvious. Having her sister live under the same roof as them would restrict his style, something he knew, yet he'd offered anyway. And it hadn't been a half-assed offer either. He'd been completely sincere.

As they neared the front door, she noticed a piece of paper taped to it. Stephan grabbed it before she could reach it. He grinned as he read it.

"What?"

Wordlessly, he passed it to her.

Your clothes are too big and after a year of being kept naked, I want something that fits. I've gone shopping with Caro. I know I freaked before, but she's cool so don't worry. We'll be gone for hours. Enjoy your mate, little hermana. Love, Paz. P.S. I want details.

She folded the note and tucked it into her jeans as Stephan opened the door. When she walked past him, his lust rolled over her like a heat wave. Suddenly, she felt nervous.

They'd had sex. Lots of it. And it had been mind-blowing. Bonding was different though. What if they didn't do it right? What if she somehow screwed it up? Werewolves were superstitious and if the bonding didn't go well, it was supposed to curse the mates for life. That was a long freaking time.

"Stop," Stephan growled close to her ear.

She swiveled to face him. "What?"

"Stop worrying." He shut and locked the door behind him, the click almost ominous sounding. Before she could think about what the next step should be, he advanced on her like a predator stalking its prey and lifted her up so she had no choice but to wrap her legs around his waist.

His mouth descended on hers with little finesse. Hungrily he ate at her lips, stroking his tongue over hers with such fervor, her pussy contracted with the need for him. She could taste the remnants of his toothpaste—sweet and minty.

Scrambling for the hem of his shirt, she tugged at it while he carried her up the stairs. After she peeled it off, she ran her hands along his muscled chest. She dug her fingers into his hard flesh and groaned into his mouth.

Most werewolves stayed in shape, but this man—her man—was absolute perfection. All hard lines and muscles and just a smattering of hair across his chest, he was the kind of man who turned heads. And he was all hers.

That made her feel ridiculously proud. Her wolf wanted to strut around and freaking preen that this was her male.

Until now she'd forced herself to keep her feelings at bay, but letting them free was liberating. She was free to want something again, to claim something as her own. Stephan was hers and every wolf and woman in a hundred mile radius was going to know. She was no longer alone in the world and that in itself, unchained her.

Her nipples pressed painfully through the fabric of her sweater. As she rubbed herself against him, the hardened tips stroked against the material, begging to be released.

Suddenly she was falling. She tensed for impact but her fall was cushioned by the rumpled comforter of their bed. Shirtless, and breathing hard, Stephan stood above her. His chest rose and fell and the heated look in his dark eyes was enough to curl her toes.

He quickly shucked his pants and she was pleased but not surprised that he'd gone commando. His cock jutted forward proudly. She couldn't wait until it was buried deep inside her. His pubic hair had been trimmed before but she noticed he'd shaved and cut almost all of it. The realization that he'd done it for her made her stomach clench. Not to mention, the effect made his cock look even bigger.

When she reached for the hem of her sweater, he stopped her. Like lightning, he straddled her on the bed. His strong thighs encased her in a tight grip, making it impossible to move her legs. Grasping her wrists, he held them above her head.

She was completely caged in. The reality of being dominated turned her on more than she could have imagined.

"This time, you don't do anything unless I say," he rasped.

She nodded and her hair swished against the covers. "Okay."

With one hand, he held her wrists in place, and with the other, he pushed her sweater up. As his hand trailed up her skin, tingles trailed across her entire body. When her breasts were bared, she fought off an involuntary shiver. Cool air rushed over her, but before she could blink, he covered one nipple with his mouth. Kissing and teasing, he trailed moist circles around her areola.

Arching her back, she tried to get closer to him. When she attempted to spread her legs, his thighs tightened around her.

His head lifted slightly. "I don't think so," he murmured against her breast. His hot breath sent tantalizing shivers skittering across her skin.

The hand keeping her wrists captive loosened and he worked a slow trail down to her other aching breast. Cupping it, he lightly stroked his thumb over the distended tip while continuing the assault with his tongue. The male was way too talented for his own good.

Her pussy clenched and unclenched with the need to be filled. She'd assumed he'd want to get straight to business and mark her but it appeared he was taking his sweet time.

Of all times, she did not want foreplay. After the rough coupling they'd had in that bathroom, she hadn't been able to get it out of her mind. She'd always thought she liked her sex a little softer, but when he'd taken her like that, almost in anger, it had been hot as sin.

And she wanted more of it.

Since he'd released her hands, she was free to do as she pleased. Threading her fingers through his thick hair, she clutched his head. What he was doing to her breasts felt amazing but unless he eased the throbbing between her legs, he was just a damn tease.

"Enough," she muttered.

He chuckled against her skin and lifted his head. When their gazes locked, there was no laughter in his eyes. He looked…feral.

And hungry. *For her.*

The dark glint sent her senses haywire. She was his meal and that was more than fine with her. His hands dipped south and in a few movements, he'd unzipped her jeans and pushed them down. Somehow, he managed to get her almost fully undressed without losing that skin on skin contact.

While he tugged her pants off, she finished shimmying out of her sweater. Now the only barrier between them was her barely there thong.

With one of his large hands, he covered her mound. Teasingly, he pushed the flimsy material to the side and played with her clit. Strumming the hardened bud with his middle finger, he kept his eyes locked on hers.

She could come simply from the light stroking and his white-hot gaze. But she wanted him inside her when that happened. She wanted their bonding to be perfect. For a year she hadn't had anything good or pure in her life, and she wanted this to be everything she'd ever hoped for. More importantly, she wanted it to be perfect for him. He deserved it.

"I'm ready." She almost didn't recognize her own voice as she spoke. Her hoarse words sounded sensual and seductive.

Without a word, he removed his hand, grasped her hips and flipped her over. The sudden show of power made her entire body light up with need.

As he clutched her hips, she was already pushing up on all fours. The need to feel him inside her was overpowering. He pulled her panties down so they were at her knees and spread her thighs apart a little more.

Her thong added a bit of restriction to her movements and when a brief thought of what it might be like to be tied up by him flashed in her mind, heat pooled between her legs. She could definitely get on board with that idea.

He ran a callused palm over her back and ass then reached between her legs. Tracing a finger over her folds, he kept going until he skated over her clit, just barely teasing her. Before she had time to protest his slowness, he moved back and pushed inside her. She couldn't bite back a moan.

She clenched around his finger and tried to push back, needing to feel him deeper. He removed his finger before bending forward over her. His chest rubbed over her back and she could feel his cock pressing against her opening. Still, he didn't try to push into her. Instead, he placed his hands over hers and feathered kisses along the back of her neck.

Apparently he was determined to make her crazy.

"You sure you're ready?" he murmured in between kisses.

"Yes." More than ready.

That was all he needed to hear. Pushing up, he placed his hands firmly around her hips and thrust into her, filling her completely. Without giving her a chance to adjust, he pulled out then pushed in again. This time with more force.

Her inner walls clenched and contracted around him with a fervor. She was so slick and wet, she had no problem taking him. Gasping, she clutched the sheets and tried to ground herself as he thrust in and out of her.

"Who do you belong to?" His voice was raspy.

"You," she whispered.

"Who?" he growled.

"Stephan." The word tore from her throat like a prayer.

The declaration seemed to do something to her. As she said it, she realized it was true. Her life had changed drastically after finding him and now they had a whole mess of things to worry about, but she finally felt like she belonged somewhere. With someone.

The harder he pushed, the more she propelled toward that edge. Her inner walls contracted wildly until that sweet release was just within her reach.

"Let go," he murmured before raking his teeth over the area where her neck and shoulder connected.

So she did. Her fingers dug into the sheets as a powerful climax ripped through her. Her pussy pulsed around him as she rode through her orgasm. The desire in her belly uncoiled with a burst as the pleasure expanded and coursed through her entire body. Even her toes tingled with the release.

Before she could come down from her high, Stephan scored his extended canines into her neck. The sharp feel of his teeth imprinting her make her cry out in a mix of pleasure and pain. "Stephan."

He growled against her neck, the sound completely primitive. The knowledge that they were bonded override the fleeting pain.

After marking her, his grip on her hips tightened as he continued to drive into her. With a shout, he emptied himself inside her and when he finished, he lightly squeezed her waist before collapsing on the bed. Instead of falling on top of her, he rolled to the side and dragged her with him. He stroked his hands all over her, as if he couldn't get enough of touching her. She felt exactly the same.

She curled up against him, savoring the feel of their bodies intertwined. She wasn't sure if she should feel different now that they were bonded. Glancing down at herself, everything looked and felt normal. Propping up on one elbow, she looked at Stephan. "Do you feel...different?"

"Yeah, I hope you do too. If not, I seriously fucked that up." He chuckled under his breath as he reached out and stroked her neck. "Are you okay? I didn't hurt you, did I?"

"I'm fine, but that's not what I meant." She bit her bottom lip. Narrowing her gaze at him, she tried to project her thoughts. *What does kardia mou mean?*

"My heart," he murmured as he stroked his thumb over her tender neck.

Oh...hey, it worked.

We should also be able to communicate in wolf form now too, he said.

"So, my heart, huh?" she asked aloud.

His eyes flashed a darker shade as he nodded. "That's right, vixen. You're mine now."

She scooted up a few inches and pressed her lips against his. All the external stuff in their life melted away for a few seconds as his hand strayed to her waist and he pulled her closer against him. The skin on skin contact was exactly what she needed.

The fact that the Council was sending their enforcer to Miami was a little scary, but she had no doubt the Lazos pack—now her pack—would protect her and her sister. Stephan's father hadn't hesitated in his commitment to take them in. In her experience, that was a rare quality. She'd loved her pack but they'd been wary of all outsiders. The Lazos' had not only taken them in, but the blonde werewolf from the lab as well.

While there weren't any declarations of undying love between her and Stephan, she knew it was only a matter of time before she told the big wolf she loved him. Hell, she was half in love with him now. Maybe more than half. Saying it now wouldn't feel right though. Sighing contentedly, she snuggled closer to him.

It would be nice if everything in their lives could be fixed and wrapped up with a pretty red bow, but that wasn't going to happen. Still, even with all the external forces against them, she felt incredibly lucky and safe in the arms of her mate.

EPILOGUE

Two Days Later

"What the hell is that?" Stephan growled and tightened his grip over Marisol's bare stomach.

"I think it's my cell phone." Chuckling, she swatted his hand away and rolled over. Scrambling for her purse, she found it where she'd tossed it on the floor earlier. When she saw the number on the caller ID, she frowned. It was a Miami area code but she didn't recognize it. "Hello?"

"I left a present for you." A familiar voice chilled her veins.

"Preston Morales," she spat his name.

"So you remember me?" His voice was low, mocking.

Of course she remembered the wolf who'd helped betray her pack. She turned around to find Stephan sitting straight up in bed. His jaw was tense, the rage rolling off him potent. She tried to ignore it and focus on Preston. He was calling her for a reason. "What present are you talking about?"

"Antonio Perez of course."

"*You* killed him? Why?" It made no sense considering they'd been business partners.

"Sniveling human tried to double-cross me."

"What do you want?" She tried to fight the nausea swelling in her stomach. Despite the fact the last couple days with Stephan had been absolute heaven, a dark cloud had been hanging over her head. Whoever had killed Perez was still out there and now she knew who that someone was.

"What I've always wanted. You."

"What?"

"I've been trying to track you for months but you're a sneaky little bitch."

Her throat clenched. She opened her mouth but no sound would come out. She'd been extra careful over the past year because she'd known he'd been out there, but she hadn't realized he'd been hunting her.

He continued, "Perez was your first gift. Until you give yourself over to me, I'll keep delivering more presents."

The way he said "presents" sent a chill slithering down her spine. "Why'd you poison my pack?"

"Your father didn't want us together. No one did. I thought that once they were out of the way we'd be together. But you had to run away from me." His voice trembled manically.

"You're insane!"

"Watch your tongue, little bitch. You've got something to lose now. Either come to me willingly or I'll kill that wolf you've been fucking."

He'd been watching her.

As if he read her mind, he said, "That's right. I know you've shacked up with that Lazos wolf. You've got twenty-four hours to make a decision. Come to me willingly or I'll get you myself." The phone died.

Her hands trembled as she laid the phone on the bed between her and Stephan. "That was Preston Morales. He just admitted to killing Perez. Said it was a present for me. Either I give myself over to him in the next twenty-four hours or he's threatened to kill you."

A dark shadow crossed Stephan's gaze. "Sweetheart, we're going to catch this bastard and put him in his grave. He just made his first mistake by contacting you. If he knows we're together, then he's in Miami."

Another tremble raced through her. "Why the hell is that a good thing?"

"He's one wolf. My family is strong and we have ties all over the city. Hell, the world. Now that he's on our radar, he's dead. I'll keep you and your sister safe, *kardia mou,* I promise." There was a dark edge to Stephan's voice that left no doubt in her mind, he'd keep his word.

Fear still trickled through her body, but she had an entire pack of fearless wolves to back her up. She was still a little scared for her mate, but she had to believe that they'd kill Preston. If the evil wolf had been half-smart he wouldn't have contacted her. Now he'd shown all his cards and it was simply a matter of time before her mate ended his pathetic life.

"I love you, Stephan." She didn't care if it was too soon, that they were still getting to know one another. She felt the love for him bone deep and it wasn't going away. Ever.

With a sigh that sounded a lot like relief, he gathered her into his arms. "I love you too."

Thank you for reading Worth the Risk. I really hope you enjoyed it. If you don't want to miss any future releases, please feel free to join my newsletter. I only send out a newsletter for new releases or sales news.

Find the signup link on my website:
http://www.savannahstuartauthor.com

COMPLETE BOOKLIST

Miami Scorcher Series

Unleashed Temptation

Worth the Risk

Power Unleashed

Dangerous Craving

Desire Unleashed

Crescent Moon Series

Taming the Alpha

Claiming His Mate

Tempting His Mate

Saving His Mate

To Catch His Mate

Futuristic Romance

Heated Mating

Claiming Her Warriors

Claimed by the Warrior

Contemporary Erotic Romance

Adrianna's Cowboy

Dangerous Deception

Everything to Lose

Tempting Alibi

Tempting Target

Tempting Trouble

ABOUT THE AUTHOR

Savannah Stuart is the pseudonym of *New York Times* and *USA Today* bestselling author Katie Reus. Under this name she writes slightly hotter romance than her mainstream books. Her stories still have a touch of intrigue, suspense, or the paranormal and the one thing she always includes is a happy ending. She lives in the South with her very own real life hero. In addition to writing (and reading of course!) she loves traveling with her husband.

For more information about Savannah's books please visit her website at: www.savannahstuartauthor.com.